CU00792880

WITHDRAWN FROM STOCK
03/04

The Cougar Canyon Run

By the same author

Shoot on Sight
Hellfire Pass
Blood Kin

The Cougar Canyon Run

HANK J. KIRBY

ROBERT HALE · LONDON

First published in Great Britain 1998

ISBN 0 7090 6288 5

Robert Hale Limited
Clerkenwell House
Clerkenwell Green
London EC1R 0HT

Photoset in North Wales by
Derek Doyle & Associates, Mold, Flintshire.
Printed and bound in Great Britain by
WBC Book Manufacturers Limited, Bridgend.

1
Drifter

Wyatt couldn't help but smile as he laid out his cards on the table at the edge of the pile of coins and bills, one by one, building them into the winning hand – a busted flush.

'See 'em and weep, *amigos*,' he said, letting the others take a good long look through the heavy haze of tobacco smoke that had been stinging his eyes for hours.

His shoulders creaked as he stretched his arms and then spread them to relieve the cramp he felt in his chest. He heard a bit of stitching go in the seams and looked down at the worn, washed-blue shirt with its threadbare cuffs and missing buttons. His work trousers weren't in much better shape but now it no longer mattered. With the pot on the table he could buy a whole new set of clothes, and new boots, too, and a box of ammo for the old six-shooter rammed into his belt. Hell, he might even buy a proper gunbelt and holster: he'd sold his a couple of weeks ago in Anaconda so he could put some grub in his belly.

Now he lowered his arms, gave the other

murmuring players a grin and began to rake in the stake.

'We gonna get a chance to get our money back?' asked one man, the local storekeeper, Wyatt believed. He hadn't taken much notice of who he was playing cards with, just the cards themselves.

'Not tonight, gents – I need every cent. I was flat busted when I hit town, sold my saddle-bags for a stake-and-a-steak. The few dollars left I gave to you fellers . . . but my luck finally turned, and I'm winning and grinning – and going.'

He scooped the money into his hat, standing now, tall and muscular and lean, that narrow, sun-dark face looking somehow dangerous even with the crooked smile slanting the thin lips.

'*Muchas gracias, amigos* – now, *adios*.'

A couple of the men muttered and looked annoyed, but one big-chested *hombre* in his late forties with pepper-and-salt sideburns called, 'Good luck to you, cowboy. Looks like you might need it.'

Wyatt paused on his way to the bar, looked back soberly. 'Could be right, friend. I'm the kind of *hombre* who has a little piece of luck and has to make do with it for a long time before the next lot comes my way. There'll be money at the bar for you all to have a drink on me.'

They watched him pay the barkeep and head for the batwings. There were streaks of grey in the sky over the mostly dark buildings of the town.

The game had gone on for a lot longer than he'd figured. Well, the results were worth the long hours, he reckoned. He leaned against the saloon wall, began stuffing the money away in the couple of pockets in his clothes that didn't have holes in them. Then he jammed his old brown hat with the ragged bullet hole in the brim, firmly on his head and, whistling, hands in pockets, strolled along the street. He glanced across at the livery stables where the hostler had told him he could sleep the night as long as he moved a little hay into the feed bins come morning.

Hell with the stables for tonight: he'd have a soft bed to sleep on for once. A soft bed and a full belly in the morning when he bought breakfast. Then, while spending a dime at the bath house, he'd send a Mexican kid to the general store to fetch him some new clothes. The boots and leather gear he'd buy himself . . . he preferred to choose his own belts. He started across an alley mouth, remembering he had earlier seen a place that rented rooms on this side of the street. As he did so, something moved with a slight scraping sound from the edge of the alley.

Instinctively, he moved his head aside and twisted his body sharply. The club caught the point of his right shoulder, numbing his fingers so that he fumbled his grip on the sixgun in his belt and it fell to the ground. By then, the attacker was at the end of his follow-through and stumbled because his club hadn't hit solidly. Wyatt put a fist into the middle of the man's face and blood gushed from a crushed nose.

Wyatt drew back his fist for a second blow, and saw that the man had company – twice over.

Two big men stepped out of the alley and he thought one of them was the big-chested, pleasant fellow from the card game, but didn't have time to be sure. Something exploded alongside his head and, as he stumbled, a boot scooped his legs out from under him and he crashed on his side in the dust. He knew he was in real trouble now that he was down. . . .

The one with the club and the bloody face was cursing something awful as he waded in, boots kicking at the drifter's back, seeking the spine, the club swinging wildly. Wyatt's old hat crushed under the blow and fell off. Fireworks exploded behind his eyes. His body shuddered to the thud of boots. Someone twisted up his frayed shirt collar and it cut his wind and he began making strangling sounds, clawing at the hand desperately, fighting to get his legs under him.

But this wasn't the first 'lucky' card-player this trio had jumped: they kicked his legs again, allowing him no purchase. An elbow jammed between his eyes. A fist made a meaty sound when it smashed into the side of his neck. And a blow with the club sent him spinning away into darkness. . . .

He opened his eyes and wished he hadn't. Brilliant sunlight slashed across them through gaps in the sides of the swaying boxcar. The sliding door was slightly ajar and a slab of sunlight fell on the straw-littered floor.

He moaned, ran a shaky hand across his eyes, feeling one puffed and swollen, the other matted with what he took to be dried blood. *His* blood.

He remembered the beating then when the

three hardcases had jumped him – and taken his winnings!

He started to sit up, but fell back with a heavy grunt as the pain grabbed his body from scalp to toenails. They'd sure worked him over, all right . . . even his fingers ached and hurt when he moved them, making a brief experimental fist. He probed gingerly and found plenty of sore places and swellings, a couple of gashes and raw spots, but he didn't think there were any broken bones. No, they were experts. If they'd wanted to cripple him they would have.

But all they'd wanted was his winnings and to put him out of commission long enough to throw him into an empty freight car and stay unconscious until the train was far from the town.

Still lying on his side on the gritty floor, a little straw blowing up against his split lips, Wyatt looked at the gap in the sliding doorway as it narrowed and widened with the motion of the train.

Distant peaks, looking bluish but with snow capping them. Way down the sides, the timberline was a meandering dark patch, mostly conifers, pine and firs. Must be climbing the sierras . . . *the sierras*! Goddamnittohell! Not this way!

Then suddenly the sound changed: the *clackety-clack* became a hollow, drumming sound and he could actually hear the rasp of metal-to-metal as the iron wheels spun along the tracks. He had a sensation of pressure against his body and the whole car rocked and metal squealed and he thought he heard the hiss of sparks. *Bend*, his mind registered and he managed to get up on to one elbow.

They were going over a long, high and curving trestle bridge. He glimpsed greenish river water edged in white far below before he fell back, gasping.

Only big trestle bridge he knew of in the sierras was the one across the Madison River, way downstream from Ellis, Colorado. If this was it, he must have been out for nearly all of the morning. Well, his belly told him he could be right. And his bladder.

He somehow got to his knees, crawled to the door and jammed himself there while he urinated, squinting into the sunlight. Behind him he counted another boxcar, three tarp-covered open wagons and the caboose. Ahead, there were two more boxcars, some cattle wagons and *two* locomotives.

He knew then they were in the sierras for sure: it was the only place they used a double-hitch . . . those months of working on the railroad in Keyboard had paid off. It gave him a knowledge of locations and timetables and signs that could tell him where he was.

This wasn't the way he would have chosen to go but there was nothing to be done about it now. He had no thought of going back to that miserable town and trying to recover his winnings. He was used to losing: even when he won. . . .

Long ago he had learnt that a drifter with troubles had either to accept them or sort them out for himself. The law wasn't interested in hearing complaints from jobless, fiddlefooted saddle-bums: any sheriff was more likely to throw him in jail or find a place for him on the local chain-gang. . . .

No, the card money was gone. It didn't matter a hell of a lot, seeing as he'd never really had it in the first place. He smiled sourly, thinking Ma was right again: she'd always told him that no good ever came of any money a man didn't earn through an honest day's work.

He pushed it from his mind. His next problem was to find grub and shelter, then somewhere he could drop off without breaking a leg and make his way to some form of habitation where he could beg, borrow or steal decent clothes for a start, for it would be cold at night and early morning in this part of the sierras. He could even feel a bite in the wind that blew through the gap in the sliding door and, judging by the sun's position, it must be mighty close to noon.

He knew he would never make it swinging along outside the boxcars so as to reach the first of the tarp-covered wagons. Past experience had taught him that usually these were the kind of wagons that carried food for the general stores along the railroad. Not always, but usually. But his injuries and stiffness at the moment would make it highly dangerous trying to get from this car to the first of those wagons. . . .

Still, if he could get up on to the roof, it would be easier. . . .

But a half-hour later, during which time he had tried to massage and exercise his stiffness and soreness away, the decision was made for him just how he was going to leave the car.

He heard them on the roof and thought for sure they were railroad detectives coming with pick-handles to beat-up on any freeloaders. He couldn't get out of the car and tried to reach the sliding door, aiming to push it home and drop the locking pin into place, but they were too quick for him.

He backed up against the opposite wall as the big one wrenched back the door, hung there against the bright sunlight a few moments and then swung inside, followed by a slightly smaller man. Wyatt moaned inwardly when he saw they were wearing faded and torn army uniforms.

Deserters. Men with nothing to lose. . . .

'Ah, shoot, Jack, will you look at what we got here?' the big one growled, scratching at his heavy beard.

'Nothin', Nate,' answered the second man. 'That's what we got – I'd say someone beat us to him, an' beat him, too, cleaned him out. . . .'

'That right, you son of a bitch?' The big one stood with tree-trunk legs braced against the sway of the train now beginning to labour on an up-grade. 'Bet you been rolled already.'

Wyatt nodded. 'Back in Noon Creek. I won at cards.'

'You *lost* at cards, you mean!' the lean man grinned, scratching at his lank hair under the greasy army hat. 'Well, all we got us is a box car with plenty of room, Nate.'

'Looks kinda crowded to me.'

They started moving in on Wyatt and although they weren't holding any weapons, he knew he didn't stand a chance. They both had knives on their belts and he thought the big one had a small gun rammed into the top of his boot.

Then maybe he had a chance after all.

As they came at him, he dropped to his knees,

threw himself towards them, grabbed the big man's thick leg, feeling the iron muscles under the worn army cloth. Judas, he hoped he was right about that gun. . . .

He was. It was a small Sheriff's Special in .36 calibre and, judging by the fancy pearl handles, he figured most likely it had been a lady's gun before these two had gotten their hands on the weapon. Likely raped her for good measure.

But he had it now and Nate yelled a warning, jumping back, cannoning into Jack. Both men went for their knives and Nate moved with the speed of a striking rattler, hand going back, blade ready to throw.

Wyatt, on his back, didn't waste breath on warnings or curses. He fired, rapidly, turning the gun on to Nate first, moving it to Jack and seeing his first shot take the man through the neck. As he fell, blood spurting, he emptied the remaining shots into Nate and rolled aside as the big man's body thudded to the floor of the boxcar.

He coughed in the gunsmoke and fought to his knees. The deserters had stopped twitching now and he tossed the empty gun aside, went through their pockets. He collected eleven dollars and some cents, a plug of chewing tobacco and their knives. The lean one's boots fitted him well so he kept them and took the big one's hat which wasn't too bad a fit after he had torn off a strip of the man's shirt and wadded it under the inner band.

He sat with his back against the swaying wall until the sun started to go down and shadows fingered the land beyond the boxcar darkly.

He didn't aim to stay here and have the freight

roll into some town where the law was waiting and find him sitting here with two dead men and a lady's empty sixgun with pearl grips sliding about the floor.

This wasn't a part of the country he particularly wanted to be in, but beggars can't be choosers – another of his mother's sayings.

So, when it was dark and the double-hitch locos were labouring up the grade still and the icy blades of the night wind pierced his thin clothes, Wyatt limped to the door, slid it open, clapped a hand on to his army hat and threw himself out into the night.

That was one good thing about being in this neck of the woods, anyway, he thought as he dropped through the darkness. At least he knew where the softest parts of the slopes were located.

But when he hit and the pain jolted through him, he wondered if he'd made a miscalculation. He tumbled and rolled and slid and dust rasped at his nostrils and blinded him so that he didn't see the tree stump.

But he sure as hell felt it. Then passed out once more.

2
'You!'

What the hell am I doing here?

This thought smashed into Wyatt's weary brain as he stood on the ridge and looked down at the ranch in the basin below. His scaled lips were pulled tight and the sweat in the stubble that had now reached a stage of a young beard, itched like hell.

He sat down on a rock and bit off a chew of the plug he had taken from the deserter on the train. He chomped and stared, not really seeing the tumbledown spread in the distance below, but seeing something way back, years ago, and he shook his head slowly, spat a brown stream.

'Something's working to fetch me back here,' he said aloud.

And he knew he was right. Hell, what strange force had directed him to Noon Creek in the first place? There had been other railroad towns just as close when he had quit Iron Butte with the lead singing about his ears. One of those bullets had done for his mount but it had taken him up into the ranges before it had collapsed and put him afoot.

By that time he had shaken the posse and he managed to get his saddle free, humped it on his aching shoulders for shade as much as anything else. Selling it at the next town had given him enough for a stage ticket to Madison Flats but he'd filled his belly, jumped the first freight out of town – and ended up in Noon Creek. Then the winning hand at the cards had all but convinced him that his luck was at last changing. . . .

He'd walked miles since leaping off the train into the night and bringing up short against that tree trunk. Yeah, maybe that's what happened. He was dazed, reeling when he came to, couldn't have been thinking straight. That's what happened . . . an old instinct he'd thought long dead and buried had taken over, directed his feet to that fork in the trail where the sun-bleached, wind-scoured old signpost still stood. Three tongues of wood with crude words painted on in tar pointed one way, north of west: *Broken Spur; Coleman Ranch; Ellis*.

The other side of the post had only a single tongue of wood, sagging on rusted nails: *Valley South*.

And, like an idiot, he'd hardly hesitated at all before starting up that trail.

Now here he was, in the exact goddamned place he didn't want to be, looking at a sight he'd hoped never again to see.

He shook his head again. Something had pushed him here to this point on the planet, arranged that beating in the alley, even chose the train they threw him on. Then picked the moment when he had to leave that same train – in the sierras he had avoided for ten years.

Suddenly he stood, spat out the rest of the tobacco and wiped his burning lips on the back of his hand. He hitched at the worn belt and yanked it up one more notch. Keep this up and he'd have his empty belly growling up against his spine, he thought.

'Well, might as well go get it over with,' he said aloud and began to search for a way down off the ridge.

He realized almost at once that he didn't have to: he *knew* the way down.

It was obvious by the time he reached the yard that there was no one at the ranch. The place looked neglected. Shingles missing from the porch roof and also at one corner of the barn, the rain-water pipe hanging uselessly. The big doors on the barn had sagged, too, and it wouldn't be long before the left-hand one pulled the rusted nails out by its own weight and sagged even further. Inside the barn smelled musty, rotten, unused hay scattered about, weathered, unoiled riding gear hanging from pegs cloaked in spiders' webs.

The bunkhouse hadn't been lived in for a long time.

He turned towards the house, hands on hips: this was the moment he had been putting off. But no longer. There was nowhere else to look after a glance at the corrals showed him only a few toler-ably fresh tracks in the broken ground. A snake slithered away under the porch steps. A lizard basking on the splintered rail raised its head and watched him warily. Something streaked away from the far end and he thought it looked like a scavenging bobcat. The door opened easily enough and he hesitated before taking that first step inside.

Then he was in the cool gloom of the place and he tightened up as he felt it closing in around him. Voices from the past echoed dimly, but he chose to ignore them, looked around the parlour.

Same old hand-made furniture except for two store-bought easy chairs whose fabric had faded and darkened in places with grime. No pictures worthy of the name, but a few Western scenes taken from magazines or catalogues tacked up, some yellowed and torn with age. It was a man's room. A gun rack, but only one shotgun in it now. He didn't touch it. Then, leaving to walk down the short passage to the kitchen, he stopped, turned back. Something hadn't quite jelled. . . .

Then he saw what it was: curtains. Old, faded, ragged, but curtains. A woman had been here at some time, but, of course, he wouldn't expect anything else. Likely there had been a whole slew of them.

Grit crunched under his army boots as he prowled the building, fighting back the memories because he didn't want to be here and yet was powerless to leave. He stood at the foot of the stairs a long time before climbing up to the floor above with heavy, weary steps.

Two bedrooms, one with spare gear stacked in it, the bed sagging under the weight of leather chaps, a saddle with a broken frame, some sheet lead that he knew would have been used to mould bullets, reloading gear including a greasy press.

Shaking his head, Wyatt went into the next room. He sucked in a sharp breath.

Yeah – this had to be *his* room! His mark was upon it – smelly old workclothes scattered around the room, muddy boots resting against one wall, the planks spattered with mud where they had been thrown carelessly. Stiff and torn slickers.

'You always did live like a pig,' he said aloud, and actually reared back at the sound of his own voice echoing from these walls. He looked at and in the bureau but he didn't find what he was looking for. He hadn't really expected family photos.

Suddenly angry with himself, he went down to the kitchen and found some food, stirred the embers in the wood range and put coffee on. He grimaced at the thick insect-tracked grease in the skillet, crammed semi-stale biscuits into his mouth, wrenched at some jerked venison and washed it down with coffee. He'd found a tobacco sack and papers, lit a cigarette and it was so long since he had drawn smoke into his lungs that his head spun wildly at first. It settled down and he eased back in the chair, stretching out his legs, yawning.

He had no business here. He could expect no help. He'd been a fool to weaken and come here.

He would have a little nap and move on – before the son of a bitch came back from wherever he was.

Folding his arms across his chest, he closed his eyes and let his chin sag. . . .

Wyatt awoke to the prodding of a gun barrel in his ribs.

He came up out of sleep instantly alert, moving

like a spooked cougar, slapping back with his left hand and knocking the gun aside, even as he twisted away and heaved the table into the man who had been holding the weapon.

The man went down with the table and utensils crashing on top of him and Wyatt was wrenching open the door into the yard before he realized what he was doing.

Halfway through, he stopped with a jerk, grabbed the frame, gathered himself and turned his head slowly to look back into the kitchen.

Yeah, it was him! Once the survival instinct had dropped enough for a logical thought to surface, he'd known who it was who'd had the gun.

The man on the floor flung the table off him and lunged for the rifle he'd had slapped from his hand. Wyatt moved with blurring speed and his boot pinned the rifle to the floor as the man grabbed at the butt. He was twenty years older than Wyatt, maybe a little more – a man in his mid-fifties. His hat had fallen off, revealing a full head of tangled, grey-streaked, blue-black hair. The dark eyes either side of the beak of a nose narrowed as they glared up at the intruder.

'This is my house!'

Wyatt smiled, knowing he hadn't been recognized yet – the beard and the dirt had seen to that. *And* the years.

'No one home when I came in. Ate some jerky and a few biscuits and made a pot of coffee. Got a coupla dollars, but if you're insisting I pay for what I ate, I'd rather keep the money and work it off.' He paused, adding, 'I see there's plenty chores need doing.'

'And they'll be done! When I get around to 'em.' The man scrambled slowly to his feet, watching Wyatt all the while, planting one of his worn boots on the other end of the rifle, making sure Wyatt didn't scoop up the gun. He bared yellowed teeth and Wyatt saw there were two gaps. 'You just git outa here. I don't want anything for what you ate.'

'Big-hearted, huh?'

The man flushed, his square face darkening, mouth opening with some savage retort. Then he paused, frowning, squinting more closely at Wyatt.

Then he reared back as if someone had smacked him in the mouth with a week-old fish. Colour drained from his face.

'You!'

Wyatt made his face expressionless. 'What the hell you mean, "you"?' Not offering the son of a bitch any help.

The other was silent, lips working as he tried to speak. 'It has to be you! That beard threw me for a bit but – you've got her eyes and nose. What d'you call yourself?'

'Wyatt.'

The thick black eyebrows arched. 'Her name?'

Wyatt was a mite surprised when the bitterness suddenly overwhelmed him. 'I figured you wouldn't want me to use yours.'

The man stared, back in control now, face hard, eyes boring into Wyatt. 'You'd have no cause to.'

Wyatt snorted. 'You still going on with that?'

'The way she played around there was no way she could say for sure who the father was.'

Then the older man reeled as Wyatt's open left

hand batted him across the mouth and sent him staggering halfway across the kitchen. When the man had straightened, shaking his head, and his eyes came back into focus, the flaring anger died as he stared into the muzzle of his own rifle held in Wyatt's hands.

'Shut your lying mouth!' Wyatt told him quietly, his tone very deadly. He saw the other shrink back a little as he lifted his big, work-calloused hands slowly. 'You were the one who did the playing around. Couldn't leave the women alone. You thought everyone was like you, so when she said she was pregnant you made out she'd had a lover. . . .'

'Not one – a dozen!'

He jumped back as Wyatt rammed the rifle barrel forward. It took him just above the belt buckle and he gagged, doubled-over. Wyatt swung up the butt, ready to smash the brass-bound wood down on to the back of the bent head. But something stopped him and, mouth tight, he lowered the gun, righted the table and set up two chairs while the man he knew to be his father got back his wind.

Will Reeder rubbed at his sore belly and slumped into the chair, his eyes watching Wyatt closely.

'You're still a goddamned hothead, I see!' Reeder said finally. Then, 'I suppose you're in trouble again.'

It took Wyatt by surprise and before he knew what he was doing, he said, 'There was an argument over cards in Iron Butte. They set me up for it. A man was killed and if it was my bullet that did it, it was in a fair fight. But he had friends and they chased me into wild country. Got as far as Noon Creek, then. . . .'

'What in hell's name made you come here? I damn well won't help you!'

'Think I don't know that?'

'Then why? Just can't help being a sneak-thief, I suppose. Figured to rob me of whatever you could, but didn't expect to find things like this, eh?' Reeder laughed shortly. 'Botched it again! Just the way you did with that stage robbery!'

'I served eight years in Yuma for that. I paid for that mistake.'

Reeder scowled. 'I can have the law on you. Or I'd be within my rights to shoot you! I bet no one would give me an argument over it!'

Wyatt suddenly threw the rifle at him and, although startled, Reeder caught it, frowned.

'Your choice,' Wyatt said, and Reeder looked shocked at the total indifference in the man's voice. He spoke quietly. 'Just why did you come here?'

Wyatt shrugged. 'Didn't start out to. Got kind of crowded over this way . . . I can see it was a mistake.'

'Damn right it was! I won't help you.' Reeder got a better grip on the rifle but he didn't point it at Wyatt. 'Can maybe give you some jerky and a canteen of water. I guess I owe you that much.'

'I wouldn't want to be beholden to you.'

Reeder almost smiled. 'Well, you didn't get that stubbornness from her, anyways.'

Wyatt waited, but the man said no more. Angrily, he asked, 'If you cared, why didn't you come after us? You left her to bring me up alone!'

'Ah . . . I should never've got married in the first place. Anyway, I sent her a little money.'

'*Very* damn little! If you'd sent more she might still be alive. If she could've gone into a sanitorium. . . .'

Reeder looked suddenly startled. '*That* was why you held up that stage!'

Wyatt shrugged. 'Seemed like the only hope – after the years she suffered. But it went wrong, too, and she died while I was inside.'

'Yeah, that's what killed her.'

'How would you know? It was the lung fever that got her – and that was because she'd had to work so hard to keep us both fed and clothed . . . me, anyway. She didn't worry about herself. That's how she got run-down and picked up the consumption.' He paused, added bitterly, 'They wouldn't even let me out for the funeral and she was buried in a pauper's grave.'

Reeder's hard face softened slightly. 'When I heard, I arranged for a headboard.'

'Guilty conscience!'

Reeder said nothing, eyes narrowed once more.

A heavy silence settled in the kitchen.

After a time Wyatt said, 'Place don't look too prosperous.'

'None of your business – you going?'

'Might as well. I. . . .'

Wyatt broke off at the sound of horses in the yard. Then a harsh voice called, 'Reeder! Get out here!'

Wyatt glanced sharply at his father and Reeder looked mighty tense, didn't look at the younger man, but started for the door, rifle coming up.

'You stay put. This is none of your business.'

Wyatt went to the window, saw three horsemen sitting their mounts, leaning on the saddle horns, three tough-looking waddies, dressed well enough, but with a kind of mean hardness on their well-fed faces that nothing could hide. Wyatt was an expert in picking their kind. He watched, frowning a little as the leader, a thick-shouldered man with curly blond hair showing beneath his hat, gave Reeder a twisted smile.

'That gun won't do you no good, old man.'

'Maybe it's you it won't do any good, Prentiss.'

The blond man sat up straight in leather and glanced at his companions, one dark like a Mexican, the other pudding-headed, with a pale triangle of belly showing above his belt where his shirt had spread across his paunch.

'Feisty old bastard, ain't he? Well, we din' come here to rough you up today, Reeder. Just to bring you a message.'

Will Reeder waited, his rifle unwavering.

'Mr Lattimer wants to make sure you ain't forgot your payment falls due next month.'

Reeder frowned. 'What the hell's it got to do with Lattimer? It's the bank owns the mortgage.'

'Oh, that so?' Prentiss winked at his dark companion. 'Now what about that, Buckshot?'

'Well, I guess a man'd know who he owed money to.'

Prentiss nodded. 'Well, I guess he *should*, least-ways! Eh, Davey-boy?'

The fat one nodded soberly. 'He oughta know, I guess.'

'But maybe he coulda made a mistake. . . .' Prentiss looked back to Reeder, still grinning. 'You do make mistakes now and again don't you, old man?'

'I know one I made – not shooting you a long time ago, Prentiss!'

The blond laughed, genuinely amused and suddenly there was a sixgun in his hand and it blasted and a slug tore the rifle from Reeder's grip. As the man snatched at his stinging hand, Prentiss fired again and his bullet clipped the side of one of Reeder's worn boots. The rancher danced instinctively and Buckshot whooped, drew his gun and started shooting at Reeder's feet. The rancher pranced as the bullets kicked dirt around his boots, finally stumbled into Davey-boy's horse. The claybank snorted and backed-up as Reeder instinctively grabbed for the foreleg as support.

The fat cowboy leaned down casually and planted a boot in the middle of Reeder's face, kicking him back to the ground. He lay there, dazed, nose bleeding.

Prentiss walked his mount over him, leaned from the saddle.

'Seventh of next month – you have the payment, old man.'

All three turned and started away. Buckshot hipped and shot Reeder's weary, trail-stained horse where it was tethered to a post near the pump. Davey-boy shot up the pump, wrecking it.

Then they started casually out of the yard.

Wyatt walked to the stoop and shaded his eyes with his hand, watching, as Reeder fought slowly to his knees, swaying dazedly, shirt front red with nose blood.

'Thanks!' he said gratingly and bitterly.

Wyatt looked at him coldly.

'Your troubles, not mine. Said so yourself.' He sighed, looked at the dead horse. 'I'll be going now, anyway.'

As he started away across the yard in the opposite direction to the trio of hardcases, Reeder lurched to his feet, spat blood, and called, 'I'll never claim you as any kin of mine!'

'Fine with me.'

Wyatt kept walking towards the distant hills.

3
Relent

What he needed was a horse. The army boots were fine, comfortable, but he was mighty tired of walking. Yeah, a horse would be fine.

Then, less than an hour after forming the thought, he had his choice of between three and four hundred horses.

Trouble was, they were wild mustangs, sleek and happy in a hidden canyon deep in the range behind Reeder's place.

Wyatt stretched out on the grassy rim of the canyon, hugging a rock for what shade it offered. He thumbed back his hat, rested his chin on his folded hands, and watched the horses below gambol and fight and mate and splash in the wide stream under a line of willows. Even if he had a rope, he wouldn't have been able to get one of those animals. Sure, he could drop a loop over the head of a mare easily enough, even drag the fighting horse away from the lead stallion – *if* he felt like fighting for her, and it wasn't likely when he had so many to choose from for his harem – but he couldn't hope to break it without a saddle. A bridle presented no problem: he could fashion one out of rope or plaited grass like the Indians, but he would definitely need a saddle.

He sighed, watching the canyon slowly fill with shadows as the sun sank towards the hills. They were some of the finest mustangs he'd ever seen, big, taut-muscled, sleek – good army mounts.

He checked with a stalk of grass halfway to his lips as the thought came to him. Then he slowly got to his feet, the stalk forgotten as he looked down once more into that hidden canyon.

'Hell, why should I?' he said aloud at some secret thought.

Then he swung away and started looking for a way down into the canyon before it got too dark. He would be able to drink at the stream well away from the herd. A belly sloshing with water was better than a completely empty one.

Anyway, he might be able to catch a small animal coming down to the stream to drink around sundown.

Then he would be nearly content . . . nearly.

Will Reeder swam blearily up through the alcoholic daze on his sweaty bed, mouth foul and raspy, as he murmured, 'Wha. . . ?'

He lay there, blinking in the darkness, running a tongue around his mouth slowly, trying to unfog his aching brain. Automatically, he groped on the floor beside the bed for the neck of the whisky bottle.

He couldn't find it, muttered a half-curse, leaned over gently and groped under the bed. The bottle was there, lying on its side, uncorked. There was a small mouthful left and he downed this, knowing it wasn't enough.

Muttering, he fought to swing his legs over the side, wondering if there was another bottle downstairs or if this had been the last one.

Hell, why did that son of a bitch have to come here and bedevil him after all this time? He'd been no more than eight, ten years old when Reeder had up and quit, chasing after that silky-haired whore he'd made the mistake of thinking was a virginal young lady from back East. He soon learned different when she had set him up and her pardner had come in and beat him senseless, cleaned out his pockets, and left him saddled with the hotel bill. The sheriff had given him five days on the local chaingang and when he'd been released he'd gone a'hunting too ashamed to return home yet.

Took him weeks to catch up with the silky-haired woman, another four days to find her pardner. Both would remember that encounter for the rest of their days.

Hell, his mind was wandering. He'd started out thinking about the boy – and his mother. He'd left them here when he'd run out and figured they'd be here when he got back. Where else did they have to go?

Surprise, surprise: they were gone when he finally returned. She'd taken only what was hers and the boy's and it was three long years before he even heard of them again.

By that time he was over them both. Or thought he was. He'd sent her a little money with a note, but she'd never replied. *Bitch*! No, be fair –

he'd been the bastard. She was the victim. *And* the boy. He knew he was his son, but pride and booze had fouled his mouth with blatant lies, destroying the woman's reputation she had laboriously built up in a stiff-backed town, forcing her to move on.

Figured he was smart at the time but he found it was a hollow victory. . . .

He was on his feet now, swaying beside the bed, all kinds of pictures from the past swirling in his aching head. He was halfway to the door when he heard the small sound from downstairs – and he realized belatedly that he had heard the same sound earlier. It was what had awakened him in the first place.

'Prentiss an' his pards!' he slurred half-aloud. 'Judas, the rifle – must've left it in the kitchen. Shotgun's no good without shells. . . .'

Reeder got out into the passage without making a lot of noise, but the stairs were too much for him in his present state. His groping bare foot missed the second step and he somersaulted and spilled all the way down in a limp-bodied drunk's sprawl, ending on his side with his face pushed into a gritty reed mat.

He moaned, one knee and an elbow hurting, knowing he was lucky not to have cracked his skull. But he sure must have let whoever it was prowling around know he was coming.

He froze as he saw the shadow moving in from the kitchen, holding his rifle. Reeder's heart hammered faster: that magazine was full and there was a shell in the breech. All the man had to do was cock the hammer and squeeze the trigger . . . and he was dead.

He sucked in a sharp breath as he heard the hammer cock. The barrel swung towards him, a little reflected light coming in one of the grimy windows, running along the blued steel.

'Christ! Aren't you something!' a cold voice said out of the darkness above him. 'I can smell you from here, you miserable drunk!'

Reeder felt suspended in some sudden limbo for a moment. He blinked as a thought stabbed cleanly into his brain.

'What the hell're you doing back here?'

'I was about to shoot you,' Wyatt told him, lowering the gun hammer now, putting up the rifle and resting the barrel over his left shoulder. 'Thought you'd've had enough sense to quit the booze long ago, after all the trouble it caused for you – or made you cause for other folks.'

'I don't need booze as an excuse for . . . for any of my actions!' Reeder lifted a trembling hand towards Wyatt. 'Help me up.'

Wyatt didn't move.

'Damn you! I said help me up!'

'You got yourself down here, get on your own two feet. I'm making coffee. Come on through if you want some.'

'Goddamnit, *my* coffee!'

Wyatt didn't reply, sat down at the kitchen table in the faint glow from the burning wood in the range. The coffee pot was starting to sing.

By the time it was bubbling and he had two reasonably clean mugs out, Reeder came stumbling in and dropped into a chair.

'Tallow dip on top of the cupboard,' he slurred,

and Wyatt located it, set in an old coffee-can lid, and lit the twine wick from a burning twig taken from the range. The flickering orange light wasn't much, but it pushed back some of the shadows.

Wyatt poured the coffee. Reeder looked around him.

'You see any whiskey bottles on the shelves?'

'No,' Wyatt replied without looking up. 'Get some java into you.'

'The hell you think you are, ordering me about in my own house?'

'For how much longer? Till the seventh of next month?'

Reeder held the cup in both hands, cursed as he burned his mouth and set it down again. 'So? Why the hell would you care?'

Wyatt scratched his sweat-dark hair. 'Honest to God – I really dunno.'

Reeder squinted, fumbled out tobacco sack and papers, made a mess of trying to roll a cigarette. Wyatt took the makings from him, rolled smokes for both of them and when Reeder handed him a vesta with shaking hands, he snapped it into flame on his thumbnail. He lit both cigarettes.

'Who's Lattimer?'

Reeder took his time replying. 'Lance Lattimer – don't tell me you've never heard of him.'

Wyatt had. The man was a speculator, but a rich one, although some said his wealth was mainly on paper and that he'd have a hard time coming up with a hundred dollars in ready cash. He had had some success by bullying his way into a freight and stageline and was working a payable gold mine. Lattimer was said to be a ruthless, powerful man. Mighty ambitious.

'Why would he be interested in this piss-ant place?'

'We go back a long way, Lance and me.' Reeder's speech wasn't so slurred now. 'There was a woman. . . .'

Wyatt made an exasperated sound. 'I might've known!' His face was tight with anger.

'You know nothing!' Reeder dragged deeply on his battered cigarette, face hard in the brief glow. 'I loved her – so did Lattimer. She chose me, but. . . .'

'She chose you over Lattimer, with all his money?' Wyatt's query showed plainly he didn't believe a word of it.

'He didn't have money then. He was my pardner. We were prospecting but had no luck. Anyway, there was an accident. She was killed . . . .'

'What kind of accident?'

At first, he thought Reeder wasn't going to answer, but then he said slowly and quietly, 'We'd busted up by then, Lattimer and me. He'd gone on prospecting and later he found a real bonanza, but not till after . . . she . . . was killed. I was trail-driving, needed a stake. I talked the trail boss into letting the woman be the cook. He agreed, but only if she dressed like a man and the crew were never told different. It worked for a while, but it was only a matter of time before someone stumbled on her washing in a river. He couldn't believe his eyes, called some of the others, and they started joshing her, took her clothes, telling her to come and get them. She wouldn't, and I guess she figured to swim to the other side and wait in the bushes till I came back from scouting ahead. Only she was a poor swimmer and there'd been rain upstream and she misjudged the current. . . .'

He went silent, burned his fingers when he sucked in deeply on his cigarette, flicked the butt carelessly towards the stove and missed.

'She drowned?'

Reeder nodded. 'When Lattimer heard, he blamed me for being stupid enough to take her on the trail drive. I didn't need him to tell me that. I was hitting the booze again by then, too miserable with self-pity even to do anything about the bunch of trail hands who'd teased her and caused it. Well, he went after them, one by one, crippled two, killed two and scared one so bad he ain't right in the head to this day. He never did anything to me, just said he'd wait. He'd settle with me some day.'

'Did he try?'

'I guess so. Plenty of what I figured as just plain *bad luck* happened to me over the years, but I got me a notion now it was all Lattimer's doing. He was rich by then, could buy anything done he wanted. This ranch is all I've got left, and it's gone down and down over the years for one reason or another. I dunno why I've hung on, but I guess it's because it's the place I built . . . for your mother and me.'

'You were never sentimental!' Wyatt snapped.

Reeder shrugged. 'I don't care if you believe me or not. But Lattimer obviously knows this payment is the one that decides whether I keep or lose the place. Somehow, he's gonna see I don't make the deadline and I'll lose everything.'

'Would you get anything if you sold out?'

Reeder's jaw firmed. 'I won't sell! I could never be sure it wasn't to someone who was just a front for Lattimer.'

'But if you did?' Wyatt insisted.

His father shrugged. 'I guess I'd clear a few hundred. No, maybe not – I don't have any stock to speak of.'

Wyatt finished his own coffee, stood and brought back the pot, refilling both mugs.

'You wouldn't see any of it!' Reeder suddenly snapped. 'If that's what you had in mind!'

Wyatt smiled crookedly. 'It wasn't. I wouldn't take a red cent off you, but I do know a way you can square your mortgage and I can make a few bucks at the same time.'

4
Rimrock

They were being watched.

Wyatt had had a hunch earlier that someone was up on the rim, caught a brief flash out of the corner of his eye, but although he had surreptitiously watched the spot while he went about his chores, it didn't occur again.

But now he was sure.

Through the dust and noise and muted thunder of the drive down from the far end of the canyon, the mustangs whistling and rolling their eyes, his keen ears had heard an answering whicker – from up on the rim. Likely the mount belonging to the man up there.

Wyatt slanted his smoke gelding through the tail end of the stream of wild horses as they piled into the brush-lined run that led to the section of canyon they had fenced off as a holding-pen. He adjusted his dust-choked bandanna over his lower face, weaved and beat a path to where Reeder was cursing a grey-streaked black filly that kept breaking loose. In the end, Reeder let it run free and hauled rein as Wyatt rode up, tugging down his mask now.

'Don't look up and don't do anything out of the ordinary,' Wyatt said quickly, his voice raspy from the days of work amongst the dust. 'There's someone up on the rim near the dead tree. I'm gonna work my way around into that arroyo, slip saddle and climb up.'

Reeder glanced at him sharply, blotting sweat from his dust-streaked face. 'You ain't got a gun! If I slip my rifle outa the scabbard to give you he'll know he's been spotted and run.'

'I'll have a gun when I come back,' Wyatt said, wheeling the smoke away, working out of the run, hazing back a couple of uncertain horses, cutting through brush after one that he deliberately allowed to run into the arroyo.

It was under the canyon wall where the watcher was and the man wouldn't be able to see him unless he leaned way out and he would have to show himself to do that.

Wyatt dismounted, ground-hitched the weary workhorse and started searching for a way up. It looked like he would have to climb it and while heights rarely bothered him, clinging to sheer rock like a fly on the wall didn't make him feel relaxed. But if he wanted to get up there, and fast, he had to climb.

So he started and to take his mind off the muscle-cracking, fingernail-tearing effort, he thought about the last few days since he and Reeder had left the ranch after that night he'd returned instead of keeping on going as he had originally planned.

Reeder had listened to his plan to round-up some of the wild horses very quietly and with more attention than Wyatt expected.

'Those fellers I played cards with in Noon Creek were talking about the big prices the army's paying for good mounts right now, clear across the country. Seems there's a big campaign in the offing to clear out Indians and owlhoots. Fort Renown is only thirty miles from here. We could get us a bunch of mustangs, break 'em in enough to drive 'em to the fort and sell – half for you, half for me.'

Reeder's reddened eyes showed no excitement but there was a little edge to his voice. 'And how're we gonna round-up them mustangs?'

Wyatt smiled crookedly. 'I came across that draw where you've hid your outfit. Six mounts, maybe forty cows in the back-end . . . you been hiding your assets, I'd say, in case the bank decided to foreclose, leave you something to start up with again.'

Reeder glared. 'Nosy bastard! All right – I ain't had anyone working for me for months. Something happened to all my crew, one by one: accidents, beat-up in bar-room brawls, just up and quit. I guess, now, it was all Lattimer's doing. Anyway, I had them cows collected in the draw, was trying to get a herd together to sell to pay the mortgage. . . .'

'You'd need hundreds at local prices. That's the beauty of these horses. The army's paying up to thirty-five dollars a head.'

Reeder sat up straight then. 'I know the canyon you mean. It's called Shadow Canyon. It looks like no one'd know it's there but plenty folk know about it. But it's hell to work. Too big. Horses've got too much room to manoeuvre.'

'I can handle that part. You throw in your work outfit and we'll start in the morning. Do you good to sweat the booze out.'

Reeder scowled. 'Have to twist the knife, don't you?'

'Just remembering Ma . . . and what she put up with from you.'

'Judas, you're an unforgiving sonuver!'

Wyatt glared back. 'Had a good teacher.'

It looked like developing into another argument for a spell, but they both came to their senses at the same time, stopped the needling and agreed to try to catch a bunch of horses and partially break them in.

'But if I'm supplying the outfit, I want the split sixty-forty, my way,' Reeder snapped.

'I'm supplying the expertise, so it stays fifty-fifty.'

It wasn't settled even yet, but they had made a start and Reeder was beginning to thaw, obviously surprised at the way Wyatt set things up and captured the horses they were going to work on.

Panting, sweating, fingers bleeding, Wyatt paused now, clinging to the side of the canyon wall, trying to breathe quietly. He tilted back his head: there was still ten feet to go. Blood was roaring in his head. He strained to hear. Nothing. No, he didn't hear anything, but he *saw*.

A trickle of fine gravel over to his right, about three or four yards . . . that would be about where he judged the watcher to be. Smiling thinly, Wyatt dug in harder with his trembling feet, feeling the leather toe-cap actually crush down with his effort. His muscles strained in arms and legs and back and he inched his way up.

He came up on to the rim beside a small bush and grabbed it with one hand, holding his breath as it shook briefly. He could see between the branches. There was a man's leg showing from behind a rock as he lay stretched out, likely on his belly, with elbows propped and field-glasses up to his eyes, watching Reeder. Maybe wondering why Wyatt was taking so long in that blind arroyo. Maybe starting to worry just a mite. . . .

So it was time to move in.

Wyatt hauled himself up with one mighty heave that set his head spinning and he saw the man begin to turn at the sound, more curious than alarmed. Then he launched himself bodily, seeing the watcher was the fat cowboy Prentiss had called Davey-boy. Wyatt had a notion that that layer of fat covered steel-hard muscle: Davey-boy had a mean look to him that somehow said he could back it up, all the way. . . .

Now Davey-boy Denney swore as he dropped the field-glasses and rolled on to his back, right hand dragging at the holstered Colt.

Wyatt hurtled down on him, left hand dropping to fumble with the man's gun hand, blood from his torn fingers making his grip slip. But then his body slammed into Denney and the man grunted, sour breath gusting into Wyatt's face. Denney snarled and fought his gun free of leather at the same time as Wyatt jerked his head downward, the forehead smashing into Denney's nose. It squashed and spurted blood and he fell back, dazed.

Wyatt butted him again and by that time he had twisted the Colt free of the man's hand. But Denney rolled on top of the gun before Wyatt could reach it, swung an elbow back that cracked against Wyatt's temple. He saw a swirl of stars and planets and fell back. Denney kicked out, one boot dragging down Wyatt's leg.

The drifter swore with the pain, wanting to dance about it was so intense. Then he scrambled to hands and knees as Dave Denney got into a similar position, scrabbling frantically to find his Colt. Wyatt came up fast and kicked him in the face. Denney crashed back and the gun, secured only in a half-grip, disappeared amongst the rocks. Denney's face was a mask of blood and it said something for the fat man's toughness that he shook his head, rolled swiftly and clawed up to his feet by the coarse surface of one of the rocks.

Wyatt was there in an instant, putting a straight left on to the man's flattened nose. Denney howled, grabbed at his face. Wyatt worked on his ribs, but the man used elbows and forearms expertly to protect himself. Then, suddenly, unexpectedly, a right snapped out and took Wyatt on the side of the jaw. His head rang as he stumbled back.

Denney came ploughing in like a loco bull, head down, arms out. He wrapped them around Wyatt just above his belt, slammed the man's body against his and then bared his teeth as he roared and lifted the drifter clear of the ground, locked hands working back and forth across his kidneys and spine.

Wyatt yelled, too, but in pain, not with effort. He flung his head wildly from side to side, struggled to work his pinned arms free. He couldn't, then, remembering the pain that still throbbed in his leg, began to kick with his flailing boots. He drove the reinforced toes again and again into Denney's shins and knees and finally the big man loosened his hold, bending a little in pain, staggering.

Wyatt corkscrewed free and continued his spin, coming round with all that extra momentum behind the blows he sank into the fat man's midriff. Denney groaned sickly and doubled-up. Wyatt grabbed his ears, yanked his head down as he snapped up his knee. He released his hold and Davey-boy Denney slammed back across a rock, spine arched.

Wyatt stepped forward on shaky legs, pummelled him from belly to brisket, poked a couple of good ones into the man's eyes, finished him with a round-house right that had him shaking his jarred hand wildly.

Denney, amazingly, took a step forward, but then his eyes rolled upwards into his head and his legs buckled. He jarred to his knees, hung swaying there for a moment, then sprawled on his face unconscious.

Wyatt leaned against a rock, head hanging, aching and sore: the fight hadn't taken long but that fat cowboy was one of the strongest he'd come up against in years – and that included the time in Yuma.

Sweat was stinging his eyes and he shook it away, but the motion made him feel groggy and he hugged the rock tightly until it had passed.

Then he spied the man's canteen beside the fallen glasses, picked it up and swilled out his bloody mouth before drinking deeply.

Leaning on the rock, holding the open canteen, he watched the unconscious cowboy.

He wondered what the man would have to tell them when he came round. And if he had been alone up here?

'What'd you do with him?' demanded Reeder after Wyatt had returned to the holding pens and told him about the fight and capture of Dave Denney.

'Tied him up after I had a talk with him. He's kind of worried about snakes amongst the rocks, but he'll be all right even if he doesn't know it. Found a dead rattler when I was scouting around for his horse – which I never found by the way – and draped it across his chest while he was still out. Think it helped to loosen his tongue.'

'Judas!' Reeder's gaze was half-leery, half-admiring. 'What . . . what'd he have to say?'

'Reckons he was set to watch your ranch. If you left he was to follow you, see what you were up to, but only to report in when he had something useful.'

'Then Prentiss or Buckshot don't know he's here?'

'Don't know where he is at all, according to Denney – which may or may not be true. We'll have to keep him here while we break in the broncs.'

Reeder frowned. 'You should've located his horse – I'd better go look for it.'

'Bring Denney back here. We can stash him close to camp, keep a better eye on him. I'll make a start on these broncs.' Reeder mounted his thin-legged chestnut and rode out towards the trail that led up to the rimrock. Wyatt examined the Winchester rifle and the Frontier Model Colt .45 that he had taken from Dave Denney. Both weapons had been well cared for. The bullet belt only required two more holes cut in the tongue to make it fit Wyatt's waist snugly.

He settled it in against his thigh firmly, feeling more at ease now that he had a six gun strapped on again. He mounted the smoke and swung towards the still-restless horses they had just gathered. In a smaller pen beyond the main one there were already a dozen mustangs broken-in enough to wear a saddle. But they needed a lot more yet, their target being between fifty and sixty.

Now it was time for the hard work again – roping a likely-looking mustang, getting it hitched to the rubbing post, winning its confidence with floursack over the eyes and quiet talk and gentling hands before the next big test.

First the blanket, then the saddle – there would be several attempts at this before a successful one, he knew – and maybe, as a last resort, he'd have to twist or bite one of the ears so as to distract the animal while he tightened the cinch. After that – well, the next step would take him the closest to Hell it was possible to come to in this life.

A step into a bone-jarring, neck-snapping, stomach-churning, spine-busting ride all round the breaking-in pen. If the horse didn't roll on him, or kick his head in or crush his ribs, or smash his legs against the rails, it might – in time – settle down enough to allow him to ride it for a few yards.

Before it started its devil-tricks all over again.

And they planned to bust fifty or sixty head to drive to Fort Renown! Hell-on-earth, fifty or sixty times over: something to really look forward to.

Over supper that night, nursing bruises and cuts, his ears ringing, head throbbing, every bone and muscle in his body aching or knotted, the taste of dried blood in his throat, Wyatt held out his coffee cup for a refill. Reeder obliged, smiling thinly.

'I better bust some tomorrow.'

'And welcome to it.' Wyatt sipped the hot java and looked across to where Denney lay bound to a tree just beyond the firelight. Reeder had located the man's horse hidden in a cave which Wyatt hadn't known existed. 'We're gonna have to watch him for about a week before we're ready to leave.'

'Be easier to put a bullet in him.'

Reeder spoke quietly, but loud enough for Denney to pick up the words. The rancher smiled faintly as he heard him struggling against his bonds.

'Yeah,' Wyatt agreed: maybe shaking-up the man a little might make him tell them more about Lattimer. But they didn't push it any more that night.

'Denney says he and Prentiss and Buckshot

work out of Madison, that Lattimer's always moving around looking for profitable deals, just sends off a telegraph whenever he wants 'em,' Wyatt said conversationally.

Reeder nodded. 'They're his trouble-shooters. I hadn't seen any of 'em in years till they turned up at my place the day you arrived.' His voice hardened. 'You never did bring me any good luck.'

'Hope I never do. Cutting you in on this bronc-busting deal is only a convenience.'

Their gazes locked hostilely across the campfire. After a time, Reeder asked, 'Did Denney say what they're s'posed to do to me?'

Wyatt shook his head. 'He doesn't know – he claims – beyond hassling you, getting you edgy. He swears they haven't had any orders about trying to stop you paying the mortgage.'

'Mighty damn queer, isn't it?'

'I'd say so.'

'Makes me wonder just what in hell Lattimer's got in mind.'

Wyatt had been wondering the same thing.

'Well, with a little luck,' Reeder said slowly, 'we might manage to get the horses to the fort without them knowing what we're about. I know these hills pretty good and I can find a trail that'll take us there without them even seeing us.'

Maybe, thought Wyatt. But he didn't put a hell of a lot of faith in it happening that way.

If Lattimer had held a grudge all this time and was now getting ready to make his move against Reeder, he would have every point covered: hell, the man had both the money and the resources to do it, so why wouldn't he?

*

Denney escaped one night in the middle of the week. He had been acting nervous, apparently running-off at the mouth with wild tales about Lattimer and the man's cold-blooded business methods: under-the-table payments to government officials; the bribing of judges during land disputes or right-of-way court cases; sabotaging rivals' railroads or stagelines, sometimes resulting in death or serious injury. At first it sounded like he was giving out information that he hoped to exchange for his freedom, but upon examining Denney's stories, Wyatt realized there was nothing that could be used against Lattimer in court. Denney had been at pains to deny any personal involvement so it was no more than hearsay.

But it had the desired effect: both Reeder and Wyatt, weary and battered from the daily bronc-busting, were taken in by the man's scared, co-operative act and somehow his bonds weren't secured properly one night – and next morning he was gone.

He had taken his own mount, though he had left the saddle. But even a man riding bareback and one who didn't know this country well, could find his way out in a day or so.

'We're in trouble,' Wyatt said. 'If he gets to a telegraph and sends word to Lattimer. . . .'

'Well, what the hell you standing talking for?' Reeder snapped, checking the loads in his rifle. 'Let's get after him.' He started for his saddle near his bedroll, stopped and glared at Wyatt, who hadn't moved. 'You coming?'

Wyatt took a moment to answer. 'He's been gone for some hours by the tracks . . . might be better we finish that bunch we're working on and start driving to the fort. We'll have fifty-six, and if we push, we can be there in two days. There's not much Denney can do in that time. It'll likely take him that long to get out of these hills.'

He could see Reeder wanted to agree, but the man said, '*If* he was speaking gospel about not knowing this neck of the woods. . . .'

'If he reaches the fort ahead of us and gets a telegraph away to Madison, Prentiss and Buckshot still couldn't get there before us.'

Still Reeder hesitated. 'Prentiss and Buckshot might be waiting to hear from him in Valley South. That's a lot closer.'

'We could still have the broncs sold before they can organize anything. He don't move, Denney could bring 'em here.'

Reeder finally agreed and, tight-lipped, they got their working saddles and headed for the breaking-in pens.

Wyatt could savvy Reeder's worry: he knew a ruthless sonuver like Lance Lattimer must have some really hellish fate reserved for Reeder, having waited all this time.

His main worry was that, whatever it was, he was going to be caught in the middle when all he wanted was to sell the broncs at the best price and get the hell out.

But when they reached Fort Renown, after a trouble-free drive, they found out that Lattimer had been one jump ahead of them all along.

A sergeant and two troopers rode out to meet them on the bedding-down flats outside the fort. Wyatt and Reeder introduced themselves, but got no further before three riders came up, reining down, and casually watched the newcomers from a few feet away.

Wyatt immediately recognized them as Prentiss, Buckshot – and a bruised and trail-weary Dave Denney. The fat cowboy grinned despite his swollen face.

'Nice bunch of broncs,' he opined pleasantly enough.

'Yeah,' agreed Aaron Prentiss, glancing at the sergeant. 'Make good mounts for your boys, Sarge.'

The sergeant, a moon-faced burly man with a scarred neck, adjusted his battered cap and scowled at Prentiss. 'You bein' a smart-ass, Prentiss?'

The big hardcase tried to look innocent. 'Not me, Sarge. Just opinin'.'

Wyatt caught the sergeant's eye and said slowly, a chill feeling beginning to form beneath his breastbone. 'He's right, they're good mounts, big and hard-muscled, just the way the army likes 'em.'

'Yeah, I give you that. Point is, though, the army ain't buyin'.'

Reeder and Wyatt both went very still. The three hardcases could barely control their grins and in Denney's case he didn't even try. He could hardly speak for chuckling.

'Had to buy me another bronc after near wearin'-out mine gettin' to the fort. Too bad you din' arrive earlier. Might've gotten one cheap from you, eh? Man! Y'oughta see your face!'

Wyatt ignored the man, watching the sergeant. 'We were told in Noon Creek the army was buying clear through to the middle of next month.'

'That's the way it was, but headquarters in Denver contracted with a feller to supply all the hosses we'll need for the whole campaign. Ten bucks a head cheaper, too.'

Reeder's voice was tight when he asked, 'Mind telling us who the contractor is?'

'Hell, no, I don't mind. Won't do you a lot of good to know, though, *amigo*. Some new company just formed by Lance Lattimer – you must've heard of him. Can buy and sell the good ole U.S. they say . . . leastwise, on paper.'

The trio of hardcases laughed out loud at the look on the faces of Wyatt and Reeder.

'Boys, you done worked your butts off, I believe!' Prentiss taunted. 'And all for nothin'!' He shook his head sadly. 'Man, I really feel sorry for you. What you gonna do with all them hosses now? No one'll buy 'em at anywheres near the price the army was offerin'. You'll be lucky to clear expenses!'

Still laughing, the trio of hardcases turned their mounts, called '*Adios*' to the sergeant and troopers and rode slowly away from the fort.

'Sorry, gents, but nothin' I can do about it. You're welcome to bed-down your broncs here for the night, but after that. . . .' The sergeant shrugged, looking genuinely sympathetic.

After the soldiers had returned to the fort, Reeder lifted his gaze slowly to Wyatt's sober face.

'The bastard's won! Denney fooled us, must've knowed the hills all along and got here fast, sent his telegraph to Lattimer. Now the mortgage is due in four days and I got not a hope in hell of raising the money. . . . I'm finished!'

5
Take-Over

There was nothing else to do but drive the band of half-broken horses back to Reeder's ranch.

Coming in from the canyon, Reeder had led them through other, narrow canyons, high-walled passes and arroyos, with only a half-day's travel across flats on the approach to Fort Renown. This had been the hardest part of the drive, for the horses had more room to spread out and Wyatt and Reeder had spent most of their time fighting to hold them together.

The drive back to the ranch from the fort was mainly across open prairie and they figured on two days at first. But after experiencing the break-aways and the scattering of the horses time and time again they revised this to three days – minimum.

On the second night, curled up in their blankets, exhausted, the horses penned in a box canyon with a brush fence across the exit, they slept deeply.

And didn't awake until the gunshots shattered the night.

By then it was too late. The raiders were in the canyon, having torn down the temporary fence and were in amongst the horses, shooting and shouting.

It took little to drive the spooked herd towards the exit – and Reeder's and Wyatt's camp beyond.

They snatched boots, hats and guns and ran for the rocks, reaching for height as the first wave of the wild-eyed, mane-streaming mustangs came shrilling through and spread out like a thundering flood.

Reeder yelled as he lost his grip, slipped back a yard. Wyatt, higher, turned and saw him disappear as a dozen horses brushed past. He climbed higher still, clambered on to the flat top of a boulder and, panting, sweating, looked down, searching for Reeder. He couldn't see any sign of the man, but, by then, the raiders themselves were coming out of the canyon, still shooting.

He saw at least six and he lay prone, Winchester levering as he got the butt against his shoulder. The gun's whiplash was lost in the general din, but the first of the raiders somersaulted over his mount's rump and hit in a cloud of dust, causing his companions behind to swerve.

They swung their guns towards Wyatt's rock and he shot another man out of the saddle, moved aim and brought down the mount of a third. The man pitched over the horse's head, rolled up to his knees, fanned his sixgun at Wyatt's cover. The lead ricocheted, one bullet striking sparks from some mineral in the rock's surface. Wyatt yanked his head back, face stinging with rock chips.

When he looked down again, the riders were past, though hipped in saddles and shooting at him still. He ducked as lead whined around him and he saw the man afoot running towards one of his companions, yelling to free a stirrup for him.

The rider hesitated, slowed, kicked a boot free, and the man running towards him reached up – and pulled the rider out of the saddle. As he hit the dust, the other settled into leather and turned his face towards Wyatt's boulder. In the pale starlight, Wyatt recognized Aaron Prentiss.

Then the trio were gone and the downed man was yelling, turned suddenly as Wyatt stood up, and fired his Colt at the drifter. Wyatt felt the slug burn air past his face and then he fired the rifle from the hip and the man was kicked back against the boulders, staggered sideways and sprawled in the dust.

Wyatt climbed down swiftly, calling, 'Reeder?'

He couldn't see the rancher and then he heard a groan, ran towards a dark shape just underneath a bulging boulder. It was Reeder. He had a lump on his head and was bleeding from the mouth, presumably where he had hit the rock as he fell. But his momentum had carried him under the overhang and kept him safe from the flying hoofs of the horses.

He sat up, dazed, looked up at Wyatt who was already moving to look at the men he had shot. The last man was still alive but unknown to him.

'Come see if you recognize him,' he called.

Reeder staggered to his feet, wiping his mouth, and stumbled across. 'Yeah, I'm OK. Thanks for asking!'

Wyatt threw him a coldly indifferent look. 'Know him?'

Reeder continued to look at Wyatt a moment before glancing at the wounded man. 'Maybe seen him here and there. Drifter. Gun for hire. McQueen. . . ?'

They saw the reaction in the man's contorted face. 'Get me . . . a . . . sawbones.'

'You won't need one,' Wyatt told him. 'Prentiss hire you?'

McQueen didn't answer and Reeder jumped when the man suddenly screamed. He hadn't seen what Wyatt had done, but the man was grabbing at the wound in his side, gasping.

'You blamed fool! He hauled you out of your own saddle, left you to die! You don't owe him a thing.'

McQueen seemed to think about it and there was more fear than pain showing in his eyes now. He nodded. 'Yeah – Prentiss, Buckshot and Denney – they said they needed three men. I was broke. I dunno the others they hired – just fellers like me, wantin' to turn a dollar with a gun.'

'What were you s'posed to do? Just stampede the horses?'

The man hesitated, dropped his gaze and Wyatt moved in on him again and suddenly he shouted, 'Yeah! The hosses an', later, some . . . cows.'

Reeder swore. 'Goddamnit! They must know about my hidden draw!' He cursed blackly. 'Lattimer's not going to leave me a thing!'

Wyatt nodded, nudged the wounded man with his boot. 'Lie back and I'll look at your wound. . . .'

The man was leery, but did as ordered and

Wyatt found the bullet had taken him as the man had apparently twisted away, slicing flesh above his kidney area, chipping and cracking a rib. Wyatt bandaged it roughly, using the man's shirt, wound a rope around his lower chest and back to give the cracked rib some support.

'You'd best rest up for the night. You've got a long walk back to Fort Renown.'

Reeder glanced sharply at Wyatt and McQueen groaned. 'Man, can't you leave me a hoss?'

'We've got to catch mounts for ourselves yet,' Wyatt said: their own horses had pulled free of their tethers during the stampede and run off somewhere into the night. 'No time to find something for you . . . those mustangs won't stop this side of the sierras now they're running free.'

'I'll never make it!'

'Well, that's your problem, pard.' Wyatt turned to Reeder. 'We might as well salvage what we can of the camp gear and start looking for our mounts. Be daylight in a coupla hours anyway.'

Reeder said nothing, didn't even nod. But he followed Wyatt away from the wounded man and began looking around the churned-up ground for anything they could salvage.

McQueen hadn't lied: when they finally reached the hidden draw where Reeder had kept his small remuda and three-dozen mavericks, there wasn't an animal in sight. But the sign was easy to read.

Three riders had come into the draw and set the cows a'running. By now they would be scattered through the low hills and once into the brush would quickly revert to their maverick ways. Reeder hadn't even had time to burn his brand into their hides so the cows were easy pickings for anyone who felt like hazing them out of the brush.

The rancher's face was drawn and grim as he sat back in his saddle and rolled a cigarette. He handed the tobacco sack and papers to Wyatt who made himself a smoke and lit both from a vesta.

'He's started,' he opined, and Reeder nodded.

'Yeah, soon as the army said they weren't buying horses, I knew that was it. Lattimer set that up, but it wasn't enough for the son of a bitch! He had to stampede the horses so I couldn't make a cent outa them – and now my cows! He's not gonna leave me *anything*!'

'If it's the local bank that holds your note, the one in South Valley, I mean, can't you get an extension?'

Reeder hesitated, then shook his head. 'One time maybe. Not now.'

'What happened?'

The older man glared and after a while said, 'There was a . . . woman! Ah, shut up! Not the way you think, damnit! *Listen* to me! The banker's niece from back East was in town. She was about fifteen and took a pocket-money job waiting tables at the hotel. She . . . developed a crush on me.'

'Without encouragement from you, of course!'

'Hell, she was *fifteen*, for Chrissakes! One night someone slipped something into my drink and I woke up in bed with her in a hotel room. I reckon she'd been drugged, too, but some drifter lied and said he'd seen me pouring likker into her – like the clerk lied when he said I'd booked the room. . . .'

'You must have some reputation.'

Reeder ignored that. 'Helluva fuss, of course, and she was shipped back East. The banker took to me with a bull-whip. Months later, they found their little angel had been sleeping with anything in pants for years. But things were never the same: I had to pay my note right on the dot; he put the squeeze on me at any chance he saw. I still say Lattimer set up the whole thing.'

Wyatt sighed, slowly shaking his head. 'Someone ought to tie a knot in your dingus before it gets you killed. All right. It does sound like a frame-up. But I'm getting out. Now. God, you're a bigger loser than me.'

Reeder looked a little startled; but covered it with a show of total indifference. 'If that's the way you want it. Too bad things didn't work out. Least you got a hoss and some guns out of it.'

Wyatt was already turning the buckskin mount and he swept cold eyes over his father. Reeder's shoulders were slumped. His mouth was drawn down in bitter disappointment. Wyatt hesitated as he was about to kick his heels into the buckskin's flanks.

'Got any plans?'

'Not yet. Don't worry none about me.'

'Don't aim to. Was just curious. . . .'

Wyatt let the words trail off and stood in the stirrups, looking over and past Reeder. They were on a small hogback rise outside the entrance to the hidden draw where they had been studying the tracks left by the raiders. Now Reeder, seeing the direction of Wyatt's gaze, hipped sharply in the saddle.

The ranch house was hidden by another ridge, but there was a swirl of dust on the trail leading up to it. There were three riders and a buggy.

'Expecting visitors?' Wyatt asked.

Reeder's mouth was grim. 'Likely that goddamn banker! But that looks like Prentiss and his pards with him!'

Wyatt nodded, having reached the same conclusion. 'I'll ride down with you.'

'Thought you had places to go?'

'No hurry. I'm curious about this.'

He started down the far side of the hogback and Reeder, frowning a little, set his mount after him.

It wasn't the banker in the buggy which was being driven by a hard-eyed mulatto with an entirely bald head. He wore twin guns and every bit of metal on his belt, including the cartridges in their loops, was polished to a high lustre.

The man beside him wore a long calico dust-coat over a steel-grey, well-cut broadcloth suit, blackstring tie at his throat held in place with a gold slide in the shape of a wagon wheel. His cream shirt was silk and pleated at the front and he wore a heavy gold ring on the second finger of his right hand. He smoked a thick cigar and the rich aroma drifted easily to where Wyatt had hauled rein beside Reeder.

The man in the buggy had a fleshy, handsome-enough face, sported sideburns and a small goatee on his square chin. His eyes were a deep shade of lavender – and as cold and expressionless as an iced-over mountain pool in shadow.

Before Reeder muttered 'Lattimer!' Wyatt had guessed the man's identity.

The cigar moved in a gesture towards the three riders that could have meant anything. Prentiss, Buckshot and Denney sat their mounts easily beside the buggy. The mulatto sat beside his boss, arms folded, hands close to the butts of his guns which were set high and for a cross-draw.

'Having a lot of bad luck, Reeder,' Lattimer said, face expressionless, voice flat. 'I must say I'm glad to hear it.'

'Gloat all you like,' growled Reeder. 'You've waited long enough.'

'Yes – and now you're finding out just what a long memory I have.'

'Well, you've won. I can't make the bank payment. You've got what you wanted.'

'Oh, yes, I usually do get what I want. But I made this damned uncomfortable journey out here to your miserable little hole so as to make sure *you* know what I've got.'

Reeder frowned. 'You've prevented me making the payment. The bank'll take over the ranch. What more could you want?'

Lattimer almost smiled, but it was a smile that set Wyatt's skin prickling.

'Oh, that's far too simple, Reeder . . . that's something you *expected*. But I like surprises – giving them more so than getting them. I have one last surprise for you.'

Reeder was white now, the skin of his face drawn drum-tight, giving him a skull-like appearance.

He waited as Lattimer drew on his cigar,

savoured the smoke before exhaling and speaking softly.

'The ranch doesn't go to the bank, Reeder, it belongs to me.'

'You!' The word exploded from Reeder as he sat up stiff as a ramrod in the saddle. He looked as if he wanted to say more, but although his jaw worked, no words came.

'Your banker took little persuasion to sell me the mortage on this dump,' Lattimer continued. There was that slight movement of his thin lips that suggested the start of an aborted smile again. 'He doesn't seem to like you much, Reeder. Something about you and a certain young woman in Ellis, I believe. Besides which, I am now one of the directors of the Colorado First National Bank, so he could hardly refuse me, could he?'

Reeder's hands were white where they gripped the saddle horn and Wyatt's eyes narrowed. He could savvy the man's mood: losing his ranch to the bank would have been bad enough, but to lose it to *Lattimer*. It was humiliating and Lattimer's savouring of his triumph was nothing more than a provocation.

'Reeder,' Wyatt said quietly. 'Take it easy. . . .'

But Reeder was past hearing advice: his eyes were blazing now as he set them on the big, well-dressed man in the buggy.

A strangled sound came from his throat and then he leapt his bay forward, clawing at his sixgun in a wild, fumbling stab.

Lattimer merely drew on his cigar. Prentiss and his two pards watched interestedly but didn't move, either.

Only the mulatto moved.

And he moved so fast Wyatt didn't even see it happen. One moment the bald man was sitting up rigidly, arms folded across his thin chest, next he held a gun in each hand, rock-steady, pointing at Reeder. The right hand one bucked and roared in a single shot while the left one thrust out in Wyatt's direction, freezing the man as he started to lift his own Colt from leather. He was fast, but not as fast as the mulatto.

Reeder reeled, clutching at his side, spilled from the saddle into the dust where he writhed in pain. Lattimer leaned forward, studying him, while the mulatto kept Wyatt covered.

'Reeder, can you hear me, old man? Yes, I'm sure you can, even through the pain. Monte is an excellent shot, can place his bullets *exactly* where they'll cause the most distress. You're lucky he didn't put it into your stomach. But I don't want you dead – not yet, anyway – just in pain enough to remember this day for the rest of your life . . . which will be as long as I choose to let you live.'

Reeder worked up enough steam to spit an oath and Lattimer arched his bushy eyebrows, sat back, and turned those lavender eyes on Wyatt.

'And just who are you?'

'Name's Wyatt.' He was watching the mulatto who still covered him with his left-hand gun, the other pointed down at Reeder as he bled on the ground.

'And just what is your interest in this, Mr . . . Wyatt?'

'I drifted in here. Reeder staked me to some grub and on the way out I found a canyon full of mustangs. He'd told me he was trying to make enough money to pay a mortgage that was coming-up and I saw a way to make myself a stake and let him get his payment at the same time.'

'By breaking-in some horses and selling to the army,' Lattimer said. 'Mmm. So your only interest is a mercenary one?'

Wyatt said nothing.

'Too bad you chose the wrong partner, Mr Wyatt. Just as I did some years ago. You'd do well to ride out and keep – drifting, or whatever it is you do. And yet I am tempted. Aaron there described to me the way you shot those three hardcases he hired and Denney has respect for the way you fight with your fists. I don't suppose you'd consider working for me? No? No, I didn't think so. You have a certain . . . look, I've grown to recognize over the years. You'd do well to take my advice and ride away from Reeder. Please tell him that I want him off my property by sun-up tomorrow. Aaron and his two friends will come back to check that it has been vacated by then.'

He signed to the mulatto and Wyatt watched critically as the man's guns disappeared almost as quickly as they had cleared leather a few minutes earlier. The buggy turned and Wyatt made the mistake of watching it.

By the time he realized that Prentiss and the others had walked their mounts around behind him, it was too late.

'Hey, drifter. . . .'

Wyatt spun quickly in the saddle, hand dropping to his sixgun, at the sound of Prentiss's voice. He glimpsed the man's face, smiling crookedly, as the rifle barrel swept around and smashed against the side of his head, spilling him from the saddle.

He was dazed and winded. He saw three pairs of boots surrounding him, and recognized Dave Denney's voice as the man said, 'I owe you somethin', too, drifter!'

Then one of those boots drove into his side and he thought his spine had been kicked loose from his back. Another blow took him in the belly. Something crashed across his head. A series of blows drummed against his chest, worked down over his belly and his legs, slamming home viciously. Something hammered at his face.

Then he was lifted almost completely off the ground by a kick to the head and he had the impression that his head had rolled across the ranch yard before darkness closed down. . . .

When Reeder swam up out of the black weight of the pain, he blinked up at the stars. Cloud-rack was scudding across them as he became aware of the tightness and burning agony in his left side. He put down a hand, having to push it under a blanket that covered him, and felt crude bandages covering the wound.

The memories came back and wrenched a cry of anguish from him. He tried to sit, stiffened as an arm went about his shoulders and eased him part-way upright, propping a saddle behind him. A lighted cigarette was slipped between his lips and he dragged in gratefully, exhaled without moving the cigarette. He turned his head and saw Wyatt kneeling beside him. They seemed to be on a ridge and the ruddy glow in the sky told him that dawn wasn't far off.

'Judas!' he croaked. 'The deadline!'

'Hours away yet,' Wyatt said, and Reeder frowned.

'The sun's rising. . . .' He broke off as he looked again.

The ruddy glow was in the north, not the east. Something harsh rasped at his nostrils and suddenly he knew it hadn't been cloud-rack scudding across the stars.

He snapped his head towards Wyatt. 'Christ, man, what've you done!'

Wyatt spoke coolly. 'Lattimer said for you to be off the ranch by sun-up. Well, you are. He didn't say in what condition he wanted to take it over. So I left it the way that'd do him the least good.'

'You set fire to the house!'

'Lattimer doesn't really want it. It's just that it was yours and he could take it away from you. Well, all he's taken now is a pile of charred timber. Too late for you to bitch about it so save your breath.'

Reeder nodded, then jerked suddenly. 'God almighty! What . . . what happened to you?'

Wyatt touched his cut and swollen face which Reeder had apparently just noticed. 'This? Lattimer's way of letting me know he's running things around here and I'd be a fool not to take his advice and hightail it out.'

'Why'd you stay and doctor me?'

'Didn't take to Lattimer. Had to do something

while I was waiting for them to get well clear of the place, so I fixed-up your wound and after dark rode down, splashed around a little coal oil and dropped a lighted vesta in the parlour before I left. You'd turned the place into a garbage heap, anyway.'

Reeder was quiet a long time, watching the ruddy glow slowly fade. 'You never did like this place, did you?'

'The place was all right. It was what happened in it I didn't like.'

'Lattimer's going to come after you. He'll know I couldn't've set that fire.'

Wyatt said nothing.

'You'd best be on your way. I can make it now.'

'Thought you might like to show me some place to hide out.'

'Around here? You'd be better off clearing this neck of the woods completely.'

'You don't get it – now *I* owe Lattimer.'

Reeder stared long and hard. 'You're loco. Not worth the risk just to get a crack at Prentiss and his pards.'

'Told you, I didn't take to Lattimer. All my adult life I've been kicked around by arrogant bastards like him. He was sure he had my number, just wiped me from his mind as no-account, figured I'd ride on out simply because he told me to. Then backed it up with a beating that was no more than a Sunday-school scrap compared to what they give in Yuma. . . .'

'By God! You *are* stubborn, aren't you? But what you didn't like was Lattimer underestimating you, did you? You didn't like him figuring you as some petty little mercenary! A no-account!'

'You going to show me a hideout or not?'

6
Stubborn!

The trio of riders smelled the smoke first, then Prentiss, leading, hauled rein, standing in the stirrups, glaring at the ridge that hid Reeder's ranch as if he would see over it – or right through it.

Buckshot and Denney pranced their horses around him.

'Can't see a thing from here, Aaron!' Denney said.

'No. And I ain't in no real hurry to see what's on the other side of that ridge, neither.' At their curious looks he added, 'Lattimer's gonna be around Madison for a spell he said – you want the job of tellin' him they burnt down the ranch?'

'We dunno that,' Denney said, the silent Buckshot giving him a cold look. 'Might've just been a grass-fire or somethin'. All I know is we ain't gonna find out sittin' here.'

'He's right there,' Buckshot said, and spurred on ahead, Denney following, Prentiss bringing up the rear.

He'd had a hunch all along this wasn't going to

be as straightforward as Lattimer figured. There was something about that drifter, Wyatt. Tough, hard as they come. Prentiss couldn't figure just how the man fitted into this, but there was something about him that made him mighty uneasy.

And the uneasiness turned to a cold lump in his belly when he saw the pile of still-smouldering timber that was all that was left of Reeder's ranch house. The barn was gone, too, and most of the bunkhouse, only two part-walls remaining, forming an angle, the timber leaning precariously.

Buckshot and Denney were waiting in the middle of the yard and Prentiss rode slowly up to them, pushing back his hat, revealing a receding hairline, now beaded with sweat.

'Well, I knew it. Had me a feelin' soon's I smelled that smoke. It didn't have the reek of burnt grass. Lattimer won't be pleased about this.'

'He never wanted the place anyway,' Buckshot opined. 'Just wanted to take it away from Reeder.'

'Well, he sure as hell done that,' Denney said, grinning.

Prentiss remained sober. 'I'm still the one got to tell him. It ain't that he's lost anythin' he could make much of a profit on, it's the fact that Reeder thumbed his nose at him this way just when he figured he had the sonuver beat down.'

'Well, he can't blame us,' Denney said.

Prentiss regarded him bleakly. 'You wanna bet? He's gonna say we should've camped where we could see the place, 'stead of ridin' into Valley South for a few drinks and a lady's company in a soft bed. . . .'

The other two moved uncomfortably in their saddles. Prentiss tugged his hat down over his eyes, prepared to turn his mount. 'No sense in puttin' it off, I guess. . . .'

'Aw, don't be in such a hurry to leave, gents, not quite finished yet.'

They stiffened, starting to drop their hands instinctively towards gun butts at the sound of the voice.

Wyatt stepped out from behind the leaning wall of the bunkhouse, a cocked rifle in his hands, the muzzle moving in a slow arc, covering all three.

'Just see what a couple of handfuls of that smoky air feels like, boys!' he snapped, and slowly, they raised their hands above shoulder level.

Prentiss's eyes were narrowed and his mouth tightened to a razor slash. 'What's your beef in this, drifter?'

Wyatt moved his head. 'I don't look – or feel – quite the same since you fellers rode out yesterday.'

Denney, who had had a taste of Wyatt's fists earlier, ran a tongue around his own split lips. 'We was followin' orders.'

'And enjoyed doing it. Now, use your left hands, thumb and forefingers only, and lift your Colts out of leather, toss them into that pile of collapsed timber there.'

No one moved – till Wyatt fired and his bullet whipped the hat from Prentiss's head, causing his stringy hair to fly upright briefly and then fall forward over his eyes.

Three sixguns thudded into the charred timber.

'Now climb down, hands raised all the time and well away from your saddle guns. . . .' Wyatt waited impatiently for them to comply, used the rifle barrel to direct them away from their horses, marched all three over to the remains of the barn. A few wisps of smoke drifted up from the collapsed planks.

He stopped a yard or two in front of them, looking at them one by one, dropped his eyes briefly to their boots, then stepped forward and smashed the rifle butt brutally into Denney's midriff. The man gagged sickly, doubled up, stumbled to his knees.

Wyatt said coldly, 'Your boots started it.' Then the brass-bound butt smashed across Denny's head, knocking his hat spinning, and sending the man sprawling on his face in the dust, bloody, unconscious.

Out of the corner of his eye, Wyatt saw movement. He spun swiftly, just as Buckshot whipped out a knife from a sheath he wore strapped between his shoulders. The early sunlight glinted on the blade as he started his throw.

Wyatt shot him in the middle of the chest and the dark man's feet lifted off the ground as he was blown backwards, crashed into the smouldering timber. The knife clattered to the ground at Wyatt's feet.

Prentiss's eyes bulged. 'Judas *priest*!'

Wyatt had levered in a fresh shell in a blur of movement and turned his attention to Prentiss after using a boot to heave the dead man away from the embers.

'Now, that just leaves you. And your boots

walked all over me as I recall. Mebbe you weren't the one to kick me in the head to put me out, but you'll do. . . .'

'Now wait a minute!' Prentiss was tense and there was fear in the man, but he wasn't white-faced scared. 'We do what we're told. Nothin' personal in it.'

'Well, here's the difference . . . this *is* personal.'

The rifle banged and Prentiss jumped as the slug landed an inch from his boots.

'Saw you make Reeder dance . . . how about you entertain me some before I go. . . ?'

Whatever Prentiss started to say was drowned in the crash of gunfire that followed. Prentiss hopped and yelled and cursed as bullets kicked dust and gravel all around his moving boots. He stumbled and there was a slight pause before Wyatt levered and fired again.

Prentiss screamed as the bullet smashed through the centre of his right foot. He fell, writhing, reaching for the torn, bloody leather, teeth sinking into his lower lip. Wyatt let him slow down and then stood above him as Prentiss gasped, 'You . . . scum! You did that . . . a'purpose!'

'Like I said, this *is* personal, Prentiss. You tell Lattimer that.'

Even through the agony, Prentiss showed his surprise.

'Man, you ain't gonna be loco enough to . . . take on someone like . . . Lattimer!'

'Just give him my message.'

The rifle butt smashed between Prentiss's eyes and for quite some time afterwards, he felt no pain at all.

Of course, it was mighty different when he came to. . . .

Reeder fell into three days of high fever in which he rolled and thrashed and sometimes raged in delirium.

Wyatt cursed him, wanting to leave and get on with a plan that was beginning to form in his mind. But although he started to ride out on the buckskin, when he heard Reeder sobbing, he yanked rein, ground-hitched the horse and went back into the brush-hidden cave Reeder had led him to days earlier.

The wound was suppurating and inflamed. He saw that some of the man's shirt threads had been carried deep into the wound by the mulatto's bullet and had set up an infection.

Moving jerkily, occasionally muttering to himself in agitation, he boiled water, heated a knife blade in the flames, turning it slowly. When it glowed cherry-red, he made his incision. The raw pain brought Reeder upright with a yell that seemed to echo forever, but Wyatt merely hit him an uppercut under the jaw, knocking him unconscious so that he could continue with the excision of the pus-producing threads. It meant leaving the wound to drain along a wick of clean rag and he had to stay and change the bandages frequently.

Three days later the fever broke, and Wyatt awoke one morning to find the pale and gaunt Reeder lying on his bedroll, looking up at him.

'I'm . . . thirsty,' he grated, and Wyatt flung off his blankets irritably, fetched a canteen and allowed him to drink a mouthful.

'Take it slow, you old fool.'

Reeder coughed, winced, put a hand down to his side. 'What's that hanging out of me?'

'Drain. Your wound was infected. It's almost cleaned out now.'

Reeder continued to stare at Wyatt and the man moved to stir up the fire and set the skillet, and got beans and the best of the sowbelly cooking.

'I seem to recollect you leaving during the night after I showed you this place.'

'That was four days ago.'

'Then what the hell're you doing here? You said you were riding out, had business to attend to.'

'It's attended to.'

'You never said anything about coming back.'

'Had some grub to drop off, and this place was on my way out.'

Reeder smiled thinly. 'Stubborn as an Ohio mule. Won't admit to a soft streak, will you?'

'No need – I don't have one.'

Reeder nodded to the sizzling skillet. 'You're cooking breakfast. . . .'

'I'm hungry. There might be enough for you.'

'Which raises the question – where did you get the extra grub? I see jerked meat, a bag of what has to be coffee, new beans . . . and I *know* we never had that much sowbelly left.'

Wyatt didn't look at him as he briefly told his story. Reeder's mouth sagged open more and more as it developed. When Wyatt had finished and handed him a tin plate of food, helped him sit up, he shook his head slowly.

'Man, you have surely cut yourself one helluva

slice of this deal now!'

Wyatt grunted, ate hungrily.

'Lattimer'll send an army after you if he has to. You'd best head for somewhere like Mexico.' The border might stop him long enough for you to lose yourself in *mañana*-land.'

'I'm not going to Mexico – I'm going to Aurora Creek.'

Reeder blinked. 'What the hell's there. . .?' He stiffened suddenly. 'You're plumb loco! That's where Lattimer's gold mine is!'

Wyatt continued eating until his plate was empty. He drank some coffee, then started to roll a cigarette, still not answering.

'You know that? You know Lattimer's mine's near there?'

Wyatt cupped the burning twig in his hands and lit up, took a drag, then handed the cigarette to Reeder. 'Up in the hills behind the town. Got his own crushing mill and a small foundry. Stashes the gold bars in the Aurora bank until he's ready to ship a load out to Denver. Does it randomly by special stage. No one knows when that's gonna happen till it happens.'

'How the hell you know so much? *I* didn't even know that, and I been living here for years.'

Wyatt shrugged. 'Went through the pockets and saddle-bags of Prentiss and his pards before I quit the ranch. They made no complaints. Got more than two hundred dollars between them. And the grub and some extra ammo . . . brought you a newer Colt, by the way. Better action than yours.'

'Where'd you'd learn to be a vulture? I never taught you that kind of thing.'

'You never had time – I was only eight when Ma ran off from you and you weren't around much even before then. Yuma taught me. *Life* taught me. The kind I had to lead because of you.'

'Oh, so I'm to blame for you being a drifter and a killer and an outlaw!'

Wyatt let out a sharp breath. 'Let it go,' he growled. 'Who cares now? But I figured those three weren't going to be giving us much trouble for a while so I stopped off in Ellis for a few drinks. Had enough *dinero* to buy the barkeep a few red-eyes from his private stock. He told me all about the Lattimer deal. He used to drive one of the freight wagons for him some years back. Fell under a wheel and got a leg crushed. Lattimer fired him, wouldn't even pay his medical bills.'

'Yeah, Lance was always a cheapskate.' Reeder frowned suddenly. 'The hell's wrong now? Why're you looking like that?'

'I was thinking of doing this job alone, but maybe it'd be better if we did it together.'

'Dunno what you're talking about. And only thing I want to do with you is to wave you good-bye!'

Wyatt began gathering his gear, packing his warbag.

'Hey, wait up! What about my wound?'

'It's healing. Let it drain a coupla days more, rest up a week or so. You'll be all right.'

'Come back here, damnit!' Reeder was panting now. 'Look I-I can hardly move without help. You gotta see me through this.'

'No, I don't.'

Reeder's jaw hardened. 'Then *go*, damn you! No, wait – might as well tell me what you got in mind, eh?'

Wyatt stared bleakly, then dropped his warbag and sat down on it heavily. 'I guess I might as well. . . .'

Prentiss and Denney shared the tiny infirmary at the rear of the doctor's office in Ellis. Denney had a severe concussion and drifted in and out of fantasy much of the time, had trouble remembering his own name.

But Prentiss was conscious, night and day, with the pain in his shattered foot. He looked like a corpse propped up in bed on sweat-stained pillows and when Monte, the mulatto, entered, he actually jumped a little, moaning aloud at the pain it cost him.

'Mr Lat-i-mer, he sent a special stage for you. Be takin' you back to Mad-i-son.' He spoke with the soft, almost hissing accent of the New Orleans cajun, dark face expressionless.

Prentiss blinked. 'I'll never survive a stage journey with this foot! Doc says I'm lucky he don't have to take it off. . . .'

Monte stepped to the bedside and flung back the covers. 'You know when Mr Lat-i-mer say somethin', you best do it – and that include me.'

Prentiss yelled as Monte threw him effortlessly across one meaty shoulder and he beat at the mulatto's back with weak blows. By the time they reached the door, Prentiss had passed out cold.

*

When Lance Lattimer entered Prentiss's room back in Madison, the lamps were turned low and the injured man rolled his sweating head on the pillow, started when he recognized his visitor.

'Thought you were the sawbones. Boss, my foot's real bad. I need the doctor!'

'He's with Denney right now.' Lattimer dusted off a chair with a large kerchief, sat down gingerly on its edge, staring coldly at his pain-ridden henchman. 'Well?'

He could see that Prentiss was in excruciating pain, but persisted until he had the whole story. During the telling there had been a knock at the door, but Lattimer had merely snarled, '*Wait*!'

Now the door opened and the angry doctor entered, going straight to Prentiss. He glared at Lattimer. 'I will not be kept from my patient by you or anyone else! My attitude will be reflected in my bill.'

'That hardly concerns me,' Lattimer said indifferently.

The doctor was stunned. 'Why, of course it does!'

Lattimer shook his head. 'Because I won't see your bill, Doctor. Send it direct to Prentiss. Or split it down the middle, half to him, half to Denney.'

'My God, man, d'you realize how much care and attention these men are going to require over the next few weeks?'

'No. And I don't wish to. That's entirely between you and them.' He stood, bleak gaze on Prentiss. 'You failed in a simple job I gave you. You let this drifter get the better of you . . . don't expect any help from me.'

He nodded curtly to the astounded men and didn't even bother closing the door after him.

7
Aurora

He sure didn't resemble the man called Wyatt who had jumped from the boxcar in the sierras and made his way to Reeder's place and later taken on Lattimer's men.

He was clean-shaven for a start. He had had a haircut and he wore new, inexpensive work clothes – denim shirt, Levis, standard high-heel riding boots, flat-crowned Stetson in place of the bullet-pocked, half-peak, battered lump of felt he had worn for more than a year.

He had Denney's cartridge belt and six gun, but he had dyed the belt and holster a darker colour, massaged neat's-foot oil into the leather. He had changed the stag handles on the Colt for polished walnut. The Winchester rifle was untouched, but he had bought a different second-hand saddle scabbard – just in case someone in Lattimer's employ recognized the outfit as once having belonged to Dave Denney.

Wyatt felt different, too. It was a long time since he'd had a new outfit and while clothes maybe didn't make the man, they sure made a difference. All signs of the beating had long since faded and he moved with an easy confidence, forking one of Reeder's buckskin mounts.

Aurora was a mighty busy place and folk didn't seem to have much time for anyone but themselves, but the livery man told him he might find work at the freight or stage company – they were always hiring casuals.

Wyatt thanked the man and strolled through the town towards the depot. The place looked prosperous, the street busy with all kinds of traffic, folk dressed well. He saw only two mildly boisterous cowhands whistling the ladies in the passing crowds.

At the stage depot, a young woman with a clipboard told him to come back in half an hour: a stage had just arrived with passengers and freight and Dallas and Russ Farren – the people the hostler had told him to ask for – were very busy right now.

He killed time over a couple of beers and then returned to the depot in time to see the stagecoach pulling away in a cloud of yellow dust, luggage tarp-cover flapping. The young woman was on the platform, studying a list of some sort on a clipboard and she looked up when his shadow fell across it. He glimpsed green eyes under a fringe of golden hair that fell across her forehead. She had a friendly face.

'Yes?' She seemed a little startled, took a long step away from him.

'Ma'am, you told me to come back in half an hour and here I am – still looking for Dallas and Russ Farren. What are they anyway, brothers?

Father and son?'

'Brother and sister.' She pointed to a young, fair-haired man who resembled her and who was watching Wyatt closely. 'I'm Dallas. What can I do for you, Mr. . . ?'

'Rawlins, ma'am. I'm looking for work.'

She shook her head, though she smiled pleasantly and it took some of the seriousness out of her face. 'This town has full employment, Mr Rawlins. The mines at Aurora Creek see to that.'

'Lattimer's outfit?'

She frowned very slightly. 'Yes, Lance Lattimer runs the gold mine. If you brush-up your manners a little, you may even find some sort of odd job – of course, it depends how finnicky you are.'

'Uh-huh. You mean like swamper at the saloon? Stablehand? That kind of thing?'

She was serious again, nodding. 'Yes. You can always pick up a few dollars, enough to see you to the next town where you might find work easier to get. As I say, if you're not too fussy.'

He smiled faintly. 'Miz Farren, I may be just about the most *un*-fussiest *hombre* you're ever likely to meet. But I already tried the stable and I'm looking for something more permanent and with more prospects than swamping out a saloon. Something that pays pretty well, enough to keep a man warm in winter. Colorado's a beautiful place, but it can freeze a man's marrow come November.'

'Or even earlier this high up,' she told him, studying him more closely now. 'So it's not just a casual job you're after. . . ?'

He shook his head. 'I've done a lot of travelling

of late, ma'am, and I'd like to get settled-in before the cold.'

She tapped her pencil against white teeth, gaze unwavering. 'Just off-hand I can't think of anything I can offer you . . . unless I give you a note to the foreman at the gold mines. They're out along Aurora Creek.'

'I rode down that way. Be even colder up there than down here. I can handle book work, ma'am. Schedules, loadings, and so on.'

A tiny frown appeared between her eyebrows. 'Oh? You've had experience at such things?'

'Sure. Some time back, I have to admit, and I might be a bit rusty, but it'd come back to me.' He watched her white teeth tug at her bottom lip and said, 'I noticed when the stage pulled out, the tarp over the luggage rack was loose – I mean, floppy – because there wasn't much in the rack.'

'There are only three passengers going onwards. There wasn't much luggage.'

'That's my point. I stopped at that dry goods store across the street to ask about work on the way back here. The man was stacking parcels for Madison, all marked for Lattimer Freight. There was maybe six, eight boxes. Could've fitted in your coach's luggage rack easy. . . .'

'Yes, but Lattimer Freight is a separate company to this stageline . . . even though Mr Lattimer leases both from us.'

'Maybe so, but maybe the customer might've appreciated getting his boxes to Madison a day or so sooner – if they'd gone on the stage. I know that I would. Anyway, the profit'll go to the same place, but it would show the stageline is being run in a smart manner.'

For a moment her eyes narrowed. 'Are you saying it's *not* being run in a smart manner now?'

He held up a hand quickly. 'Whoa! Just giving you an example. I dunno how Lattimer thinks. It mightn't impress him at all. But if I was running things here, I'd look for any kind of freight to fill up the empty spaces in my stages. . . .'

She let her lips soften slowly. 'You seem intent on working for this stageline, Mr Rawlins. Is there any special reason for it?'

He shrugged, grinned, looking almost boyish for a moment, but the hard years showed through quickly enough. 'I hadn't seen you before, ma'am.'

He let it hang and she stared at him uncomprehendingly at first, then coloured, but only momentarily. 'Don't be sassy! Mr Lattimer has a leasing arrangement with us for the stageline, but we are still autonomous. Profit-sharing is complicated. Any extra dollars we can make are most welcome. Now, which stagelines have you worked for?'

Wyatt sobered. 'Was a long time ago. In Arizona, I was with Mojave Stagelines, later the Prescott-Whipple line. New Mexico, well, I was only with one down there, Butterfield's. . . .' His only contact with the Butterfield Line had been when he had attempted to hold-up the stage when he'd been eighteen years old, but he *had* studied the schedules first. . . .

'All now defunct,' the girl said flatly, and he knew she meant there was no chance of her checking up on him. 'I'll have to discuss this with my brother. Can you come back here around sundown, Mr Rawlins? We might have something for you then.'

He nodded. 'OK. If I don't find anything else that suits me, I'll be here.'

She flared. 'We're not begging you to come work for us!'

'No, ma'am, and I ain't begging *you* neither.'

He smiled politely and walked back down the street. She watched him go and the fair-haired young man who had changed the stage teams came out of the office, wiping his hands on a rag. He was in his very early twenties and trying hard to seem mature. 'That ranny looks like a hardcase to me, Sis.'

She laughed. 'He's only looking for a warm berth to see him through the winter – an inside job. He does seem to have some small knowledge of stage and freight lines. And he *is* pretty sharp.'

Russ Farren scowled. 'We don't need anyone else, Sis. We're shavin' profits pretty close as it is.'

'I know, Russ, but I have a feeling he might bring us something useful. We have until sundown to think about it, anyway.'

'Not me. Far as I'm concerned, I ain't interested in hirin' no hardcase.'

But when Wyatt returned to the stage depot just before sundown, the town blotched with shadows from the high sierras, here and there splashed with red or gold, the girl and Russ Farren met him at the door and she made the introductions.

Russ took Wyatt's proffered hand only after a deliberate hesitation, shook briefly, nodding jerkily. 'Tell you right now, Rawlins, this ain't my idea. My sister figures you know a thing or two that might earn us an extra dollar so we'll give you a month's trial. Clerk's wages, nothin' more nor less. You prove yourself, mebbe we'll see our way clear to lift your wages and put you on permanent. No promises.'

'Plain enough.' Wyatt was mildly amused: this kid trying to sound tough and experienced, the words obviously having been learned by rote. 'Have to tell you, my spotting that space for extra freight on the stage was a fluke.'

'But it made sense,' Dallas said, and even smiled a little.

Russ remained sober. 'You be here at six in the mornin'. Night-run stage hits the depot at six-thirty. We'll spend that half-hour showin' you what we want done.'

Wyatt nodded. 'Thanks. I'll be here.'

They watched him stroll away with that easy stride.

'That's one hard *hombre*, Sis. Reckon he needs watchin'.' Russ glanced sharply at his sister. 'But not too close – you just remember Mr Lattimer is startin' to show real interest in you now.'

She sobered abruptly.

'How long am I goin' to be usin' one of these things?' growled Aaron Prentiss, leaning one hand on the bench and waving the padded crutch at the doctor.

'A couple of weeks – then you can graduate to a cane.'

Prentiss glowered at the medico. ' "Graduate"?

Hell, what I want to graduate to is walkin' around without any goddamn stick at all!'

The doctor lifted a patient hand. 'Give it time, Aaron. You're lucky you still have your foot. Don't push too hard and it'll be all right. If you try to hurry things along, the bones won't knit as they should and you'll need a stick for the rest of your life.'

Prentiss twisted his mouth. 'I do it your way, and all I do is walk with a limp for the rest of my life! Gimpy Prentiss!'

The doctor pulled at his lips with thumb and forefinger. 'Aaron, you don't seem to realize just how lucky you are. Man, you almost lost that foot. Think how much worse it would be, getting around permanently on crutches. . . .'

Prentiss swore. 'What I'm thinkin' about, Doc, is how quick I can get after the son of a bitch who did this to me!'

The sawbones sighed. 'Nothing will change, Aaron. You don't even know where he is. But if you wish to be able to get about with a minimum of discomfort, you'd be wise to do as I say.'

The doctor started to leave, snapping his bag closed as he made for the door. He paused as Prentiss spoke again.

'How about the bill for all this, Doc?'

The man shook his head slowly. 'I'm afraid Mr Lattimer refuses to pay it. It looks like you and Denney will have to find the money, Aaron. I'm sorry. I can pare it down a little, but I can't afford to forget it completely.'

Prentiss cut in harshly. 'You done a lot for both of us these past coupla weeks, Doc. We'll see you ain't left short.'

The medic nodded and continued on his way out. Prentiss hooked the crutch under one arm and tried a couple of tentative steps. It took him a few minutes to find a rhythm and then he hobbled next door to Dave Denney's room.

The fat cowboy still wore a bandage around his head, but his eyes seemed more in focus now than previously. For a time there he hadn't even been able to remember his own name – a result of concussion, according to the doctor. But Denney seemed OK now, although he spoke a little more slowly and at times seemed a bit vague.

'Hey, Aaron! You're managin' pretty good, *amigo*!'

Prentiss grunted. 'Doc tell you Lattimer won't meet our bills?'

Denney nodded, rubbing lightly at his bandage. 'Piker! Hell, I dunno where I'm gonna find the money!' Denney sounded really concerned.

'We'll get it somewheres. Doc's been good to us – I'm gonna ask Lattimer myself.'

Denney looked alarmed. 'He'll kick your butt outa his office!'

'Mebbe – but he *should* pay, goddamnit!'

'Yeah, he should, but. . . .'

Prentiss swore bitterly: a lot hung on that little word, *but*.

Reeder was using an abandoned miner's hut at the far end of a narrow arroyo where a small waterfall tumbled down from the slope above. Ferns and a few lilies grew around the edge of the pool with cat-tails, and frogs garped at night.

Birds called in the trees up the slope. It was a pleasant place and Reeder had made himself a fishing pole, hunted up some worms and tried his luck in the larger pool downstream.

Something had nibbled the bait away although he hadn't hooked anything. Yet. He aimed to keep trying.

His wound was almost healed now although his ribs were still sore and once in a while he felt light-headed if he moved too fast or exerted himself. But, all in all, he was making good progress and figured another week or so and he would be back to more or less normal. His appetite was sure returning, anyway, and he had him a hankering for fish, was determined to catch a bass or trout or *something* with tail and fins before too many days passed.

He was trying again one afternoon when he heard the signal from around the bend in the arroyo. It was the shrill whistle of a quail: they had agreed upon this bird call because it was loud and penetrated well, could give warning well in advance of a rider's appearance.

So Wyatt wasn't surprised when he rode in on the old shack which Reeder had repaired in a couple of places and saw no sign of the man; Reeder was a careful type, always had been.

Then he appeared from behind a low rock on a small ridge, rifle in hand. 'You cut that whistle kinda short.'

'Dry mouth.' Wyatt watched his father pick his way down the slope, leaned his hands on the saddle horn. 'No other visitors?'

Reeder shook his head. 'Told you this was an

isolated place,' he said a little shortly. 'Never was any gold up here and once folk realized it no one ever bothered coming back. Wasn't sure it was you in them clothes. Recognized the buckskin first. . . .'

'Well, no one in Aurora ought to know me, but I figured new clothes, haircut and shave might help make sure I wasn't recognized.'

'Better climb on down, I s'pose. I got coffee left.'

Wyatt dismounted, handed Reeder a sack heavy with supplies. The man grunted, set it down and began to make coffee, stirring up the fire's embers.

'I'm working for the stageline.'

Reeder snapped his head up. 'Thought it was the freightline you wanted to get a job with?'

'Sort of combined . . . freightline job would've been working the wagons. This one, I'm in on the schedules for both stage and freight. That's a lot better for what we want.'

He went on to tell Reeder how he had come by the job. 'First four days've gone all right. The girl seems to like me well enough, but her brother don't trust me.'

'Why?'

Wyatt shrugged. 'Dunno. Seems mighty protective of the sister, though.'

Reeder arched his eyebrows. 'You sparkin' her?'

'Hell, no!'

Reeder pursed his lips. 'Maybe you'll need to – ought to keep it as an option.'

Wyatt's look was sharp and sober. '*You* would, of course.'

'Sure. Only makes sense.'

Wyatt shook his head. 'You'd convince yourself that way. We ought to have something in two, three weeks.'

'That long!'

'What's the hurry? The ranch is gone. We can afford to get this thing right, take our time.'

'Longer you work there, the better the chance of someone recognizing you.'

'Not very likely, but point taken.' He watched Reeder drop a handful of coffee grounds into the pot and stand it on a flat stone at the edge of the flames. 'You seem kind of unsure about all this.'

Reeder hesitated. 'I've done some wild things in my time, but I never stole anything worth a damn. This is all new to me.' He glared suddenly. 'Not to you, though!'

'No.' There was a lot of defiance in that one word. 'If you don't want to do it, then don't. I can manage alone. Not as good as with both of us, but. . . .'

His father's face was suddenly determined. 'No. I said I'd do it and I will. It's afterwards I'm not sure about . . . I've never been on the run before.'

'Nothing to it.'

Reeder's eyes narrowed. 'You'd know.'

8
Suspicion

Lance Lattimer glanced up as Monte, the mulatto, opened the door of the elaborate office. Sunlight reflected from the man's polished yellow dome.

'They's here. . . .'

Lattimer's mouth tightened as he continued to write in his ledger, finished, blew on the ink and sat back in his velvet-padded chair, hooking his fingers across his midriff. He nodded and Monte disappeared.

When the door opened again, the mulatto stood to one side and Prentiss came in, using his crutch, followed by a tense-looking Denney.

Lattimer lifted a forefinger and flicked it in their direction as Monte closed the door and leaned his wide shoulders against it, arms folded across his chest.

'You're using that thing pretty good, Aaron.'

Prentiss clumped across the room to stand just in front of the enormous desk. Denney stopped about mid-way, turning his hat between his pudgy hands: he looked anxious, yet determined, and

Lattimer narrowed his eyes slightly when he saw this.

'You boys look a lot better than when I saw you last. But, are you sure you're ready to go back to work?'

Lattimer's words made Prentiss blink and Denney sucked in a sharp breath. Prentiss leaned on his crutch, cleared his throat.

'No, we ain't ready to go back to work yet, boss, but . . .'

'Then what're you doing here?' Lattimer asked coldly, flicking his gaze from one man to the other.

'Well . . . um . . . the doc says we're gonna have to pay his bill. . . .'

'Yes, yes. Of course. After all, he treated you, didn't he?'

'Sure, but, well, we figured as we was workin' for you at the time we got hurt, you—' He paused, but Lattimer continued to glare, not giving him any help at all. 'You should oughta pay the bills for us.'

'That's what you think, is it?' Lattimer moved his gaze to Denney who dropped his eyes quickly. 'Well, it's not the way it works, Aaron. I gave you a simple job to do; you botched it. In other words, you made the mistake, you pay for it. Now, anything else?'

Prentiss moved uneasily on his crutch. 'Yeah, there's somethin' else!' Prentiss sounded breathless but was trying to work up his anger. 'We've worked for you for four, five years – we've always done what you wanted and done it well. We don't think it's fair we should have to pay the sawbones.'

Lattimer let the words drift away, waited, looking with eyebrows arched from one man to the other. He spread his hands abruptly. 'That's it? You've finished?'

Prentiss didn't know what else to say and he could tell he wasn't going to get any help from Denney, so he nodded jerkily.

Lattimer eased forward in his chair, resting his elbows on the edge of the desk, shaking his head slowly.

'It's not my policy to encourage stupidity in my men, and you two were stupid. You even got Buckshot killed. No. The doctor's bill is your problem. And that's an end to it.'

Prentiss felt a flush of anger. 'Hell, even a hard-nosed rancher pays the bills when one of his cowpokes gets hurt on the job!'

Lattimer's face hardened even more. 'Aaron, this whole thing is boring me. I can see you're going to be a pain in the butt so the best thing I can do is terminate your employment.' He saw Prentiss start and Denney frown puzzledly, not quite sure of the words. Lattimer spread his hands again. 'You want it plainer – you're fired. I can pick up a dozen knotheads like you just by snapping my fingers. See them out, Monte.'

'Now, wait a minute!' Prentiss started to lean across the desk. Monte was at his side in an instant, kicking the supporting crutch away.

Prentiss grunted in pain as he fell to the carpet. The mulatto leaned down and helped him up, even picked up the crutch and stuck it under his arm again. He held on to that arm, looking into Prentiss's face.

'You be going now, Aaron. You, too, Davey.'

Denney ran a tongue around his lips and merely nodded, edging back towards the door. Lattimer was already writing in his ledger again.

'You owe us some money!' Prentiss shouted. 'We done jobs for you we ain't been paid for yet!'

Lattimer looked up slowly. 'Monte, see they get what's coming to them.'

'It be done, boss.'

Monte urged them out of the office and along a narrow passage to a door that led to a flight of outside stairs. He stopped them on the landing.

'Gents, I dunno if you savvied what Mister Latt-i-mer say, but I make it straight for you.' He took Prentiss's arm and felt the man pull back as he tugged him towards the top of the steep flight of stairs. Teeth flashed whitely in the dark face.

'Aaron, you beginnin' to unnerstand, I think. I s'posed to throw you both down these here stairs, but I think mebbe the boss should oughta pay the medicine man, too. So, you behave an' you walk down. You make trouble for me, and we find out if you can fly. . . .' The teeth flashed again. 'You be smart now, eh?'

Prentiss was pale and breathing fast. No one in their right mind wanted to tangle with Monte. He was being given a chance and he knew he'd better damn well take it or he'd be getting around in a wheelchair, not just with the aid of a crutch or walking stick.

'I'm goin'!' Denney said quickly, shouldering past and starting down the stairs, holding to the rickety rail.

Monte smiled at him and looked at Prentiss.

'You manage, or you want some help?'

'I'll manage!' Prentiss said quickly, starting forward awkwardly. 'And, Monte. . . ? *Gracias, amigo*!'

'You be smart now – don't bother Mister Latt-i-mer no more.'

Prentiss didn't answer as he made his way down, almost falling a couple of times.

Well, maybe they'd just see about that last part. He had money to collect and he aimed to do just that. *Some way*!

Dallas Farren glanced up from working on her schedules to where Wyatt sat at a small corner shelf held up by ropes. It was a foldaway desk of sorts and small, yet he seemed to have organized himself quite well.

There were papers and books he needed to refer to but he had managed to get them all stacked neatly enough within easy reach and still have enough room to write and calculate.

He was good at figures although he claimed to have had little traditional education.

'My mother came from a good family,' he told her one day. 'She had a governess for a time and after she married my father and they moved West, well, she taught me what she could, even after. . . .'

He had paused then and Dallas, consumed with curiosity at the reluctance in his voice to continue, had asked, 'After what, Jim?'

He had taken the name of Jim Rawlins and sometimes was slow to answer to the Christian name. Now he shrugged.

'She left my father, brought me up alone – sent me to school when she could. When she couldn't, she bought books and taught me out of them. Even when she was . . . mighty ill.'

Dallas felt a sympathy for this man although it was obvious he wasn't a man who sought such feelings in others.

'She must've been a remarkable woman.'

He nodded. 'Had a hard life. Didn't care how hard it was on her, long as I had what I needed. . . .' Then he had shaken himself out of that mood and given her a crooked smile. 'Taught me to be neat and tidy, too, or I found out what a carpet-beater felt like across my backside!'

'Well, the lesson seems to have paid off.'

Now, she watched his pencil fly up and down a column of figures. She always checked his answers, of course, but there was never any need: she hadn't found one mistake yet.

'Jim, you've been here over two weeks now but you haven't asked for any time off. . . .'

He glanced across at her and shrugged. 'Nothing much to take time off for. Maybe a little later I'll take a couple of days if it's OK.'

'Just say when.'

He nodded his thanks, hesitated, then lifted a pink paper and held it out to her.

'This one – looks like an unscheduled stage-run. I can't find a duplicate anywhere on the tables.'

She reached for it quickly and almost snatched it from his grip. She saw his start of surprise, quickly smiled.

'I'm sorry. That shouldn't have gone to you. I

usually handle these pink slips exclusively. I should have told you.'

He continued to look at her. 'Well, I picked it up with the other lading slips and schedules. I'd never seen one that colour before but I didn't know it was special.'

'Well, yes. Yes, it is a special run. Russ and I usually make the arrangements.'

'Do I get to know about it? I mean, for sometime in the future when I might have to handle it?'

She shook her head, sunlight glinting from the golden hair. 'No, Jim . . . only Russ or myself will ever handle these arrangements.'

He turned back to his own papers, saying casually, 'Must be mighty important.'

'It is. Jim, I want to tell you that you're doing fine work. We're both pleased. Your method of using available space on the stages for small freight items is already starting to pay off . . . you have a natural knack for this kind of thing.'

'Thanks.'

She seemed as if she would say more, but as he was already juggling more figures, she returned to her own work, smoothing out the pink slip, recognizing Lance Lattimer's neat but cramped handwriting.

'Maybe I could take a day off this Friday?' Wyatt suddenly asked, bringing her head up sharply. And before she could reply, he added, 'Maybe you could, too. . . .'

Dallas went very still. 'I'm not quite . . . sure what you mean by that.'

'Thought you might like to show me some of the country hereabouts. We could take a lunch with us. Mrs O'Mara in the rooming-house where I stay said if ever I wanted one she'd make one up for me.'

Dallas smiled. 'Charming the old Irish widow, too, are you?'

'Too?'

She flushed a little. 'I-I really don't think I could take time off this week, Jim. Thanks for asking. You let me know if you want Friday off for sure and I'll try to arrange it.'

'It's not important – if you can't make it.'

Now how did he mean that? Did he mean it really didn't matter if she couldn't make it? Or did he mean having Friday off wasn't important to him if she wasn't able to take it off with him. . . ?

Oh, she was being foolish, she told herself.

And when she looked up and saw Russ standing in the office doorway, she started.

He was watching Wyatt and her brother's face was murderous. . . .

Mrs O'Mara was a fine cook but she tended to make solid dumplings to go with her traditional Irish stew. Wyatt had learned to take a walk after the double helping she always insisted he ate, before going to bed and trying to sleep with the heavy doughball resting in his belly.

He strolled out by the river usually, sometimes stopping on the small arched wooden bridge that spanned it at the northern end of Main, smoking a cigarette while he watched the play of starlight or the moon on the rippling waters that had their source high in the mountains behind the town.

He was known around Aurora now and other

folk out for evening strolls nodded to him, some offering a brief formal greeting.

Tonight, he leaned on the rails and smoked his cigarette slowly, looking down into the flowing waters. But he wasn't really seeing them.

What he was seeing was that pink slip that he had never been meant to see. He had innocently picked it up with other lading bills and schedules, and grain-store accounts. He had only glanced at it in passing before deciding he would have to ask advice about it.

There was a date – Saturday the eleventh, about a week away. He thought there had been a time, too, but couldn't remember. But two words did stand out in his memory: Cougar Canyon.

He had never heard of it and later had made a point of looking at the detailed ordnance map pinned to the despatch-office wall, but couldn't find the name anywhere.

Afterwards, of course, he had asked Dallas about the slip and she had taken it from him – snatched it from him. So, he figured, there was something important about it and tried to recall anything else he had seen.

A name – Bancroft? Bannerman? No, Bancroft.

The writing had been cramped and he had no more than glanced at it, hadn't really separated the words.

He finished his cigarette, flicked the stub into the river and started back up the other side of the street.

He paused at store windows, idling, filling in the time before returning to the rooming-house and an early bed. He could go have a few drinks, maybe a game of cards . . . but it didn't appeal to him, somehow.

He was passing the bank building, turned to cross the street, waiting for a slow-moving wagon to pass first. As he was about to take a step down off the walk, he paused, turned quickly back towards the bank, looking at the darkened front window with the blind drawn behind it.

There were words on the window in gold paint:

AURORA CENTRAL BANK – GOLD DEPOSITORY – CATTLEMEN'S LOANS – LAND FINANCE ARRANGEMENTS

And underneath in smaller, though prominent, lettering:

PRESIDENT (PRO TEM) A.L. BANCROFT

He was almost back at the rooming-house when two men making their way towards him along the boardwalk, lurched into him, sending him staggering.

'Whoa, fellers, hold it!' Wyatt said affably enough.

But one of the men snarled, 'Who you tellin' to "hold it", *feller*?'

Wyatt stiffened, seeing the man's companion moving around a little to his left. Instinct took over: the collision had been deliberate; these men wanted trouble.

As the one who had spoken stepped in belligerently, Wyatt stepped forward to meet him, taking the man by surprise. He kicked this one brutally in the shins and the man howled, snatched at his throbbing leg and spilled sideways off the walk.

The second man swore and came in fast, palming up what Wyatt thought was a sixgun but later found out was a hardwood billy studded with short, blunt nails.

Not that it mattered. Wyatt went in under the swinging arm, ripped a fist into the man's midriff and the force of the blow lifted him six inches off the ground. He dropped his weapon and grabbed his mid-section, falling to his knees. Wyatt kicked him in the face and put the man out of it, before spinning back to the first attacker.

This man was limping, but the pain in his torn shin drove him wild and he surged in to meet Wyatt. He took two blows from Wyatt's fists in the face but barely flinched, such was his anger. Then he lunged at the drifter, hooked him under the ribs, thumped him on one ear, and sent him to his knees with a blow to the back of the neck.

The world spun dizzily as Wyatt put down a hand to keep from falling on his face, shook his head to clear it. Fingers swept off his hat, twisted in his hair, yanked his head around to meet a bunch of hard knuckles.

He went down and immediately the boots started thudding into his ribs. He rolled off the walk into the gutter, throwing his arms across his head to shield it. The man was still on the attack and cursing him now, stomping at his face.

Wyatt caught the boot in both hands, twisted, heaved the man off, setting him staggering. Wyatt came up with his head roaring, stumbled, dodged a kick that whistled past his ear, and then butted his attacker in the midriff. The man's breath gusted out and it stopped him in his tracks.

Wyatt twisted up the front of the dirty shirt, pulled him in close and shook him. The man's head rocked back and forth on his shoulders.

'What's it all about, you son of a bitch?' Wyatt panted, still shaking him. 'Who set you on me?'

The man curled a bloody lip and looked as if he was going to spit in Wyatt's face. He brought up a knee solidly and the man lifted clear off the ground as his testicles crushed and he moaned sickly, sagging. Wyatt flung him contemptuously into the gutter, lunged at the second man who was just staggering upright, both hands covering his bloody face.

Wyatt slammed him against a clapboard wall, pinned him there with one hand on his throat.

'Who paid you to jump me?'

When the man didn't answer, he tightened his grip and there were strangled sounds and feeble gropings until at last he eased up the pressure and the man gagged, retched, then said feebly,

'Russ . . . Farren.'

Wyatt jerked an elbow into the man's face and let him fall. . . .

The batwings burst open and the smoke-hazed bar fell silent as if someone was laying a blanket over the big room, bit by bit.

Slowly, all heads turned towards the doors and they saw the newcomer to town standing there, Jim Rawlins, holding two bloody and barely conscious hardcases, one in each hand. He looked around the room, spotted Russ Farren standing stiffly beside a corner table, having risen from his chair, staring towards the batwings.

Wyatt moved forward slowly and men made way for him, some even pulling their chairs out of his path. He dragged the men with him, their boots leaving wavering twin trails in the layer of sawdust on the floor. Wyatt's cold stare held to Farren's pale, taut face as he approached, stopped a couple of yards in front of the freighter and let the moaning men drop.

'Yours.' Flat, no argument.

Farren's gaze went to the hardcases and he stared silently before lifting his head with an effort and looking at Wyatt.

'No. I've hired 'em from time to time when we needed a hand at the depot, that's all. They don't work regular for me.'

'You hired 'em tonight to jump me.'

Farren shook his head, started to form the words, 'You're a liar,' but something warned him and stopped him in time.

'Careful, Russ,' Wyatt warned quietly.

Russ Farren licked his lips. 'Why . . . why would I want you beat-up?'

'I dunno, but you're about to tell me.'

'Like hell!'

Wyatt smiled coldly and stepped forward and the barkeep shouted to one of the drinkers, 'Get the sheriff.'

'We won't need the law,' Wyatt said, without looking around and the man who had been about to leave the bar, hesitated, looked sheepishly at the 'keep and turned back to his half-finished beer. Russ Farren had backed up against the wall now and his nostrils were pinched, hands flat against the planks.

'I ain't scared of you, Rawlins!'

'Not yet.'

Wyatt crowded the man relentlessly, using his body to hold the man there and his left fist moved barely six inches and Farren gasped, lifted to his toes before he realized that the fist had stopped right against his midriff without doing any damage. Wyatt had pulled the blow. He sucked in his belly frantically.

'Next one travels all the way.'

They held gazes for a few moments and then Farren's jaw suddenly thrust out. 'She's too good for you, damn you!'

Wyatt felt himself blink, startled. 'What. . . ?'

'My sister! You're nothin' but a damn drifter! You stay away from her! She's got prospects! Mr Lattimer himself is interested in her . . . so you'd do well to stay right away from her. Or maybe he'll do worse than send a couple of cheap hardcases after you!'

Wyatt continued to glare at the man, slowly shook his head. 'Well, I'll be damned,' he said quietly, turned and walked out.

9
Mystery Run

When Wyatt went to work the next morning, he was surprised to see Dallas Farren waiting for him at the side entrance to the depot used by employees. She was dressed in a navy-blue full-length dress with three-quarter sleeves that had wide white cuffs turned back on themselves. With a white belt about her waist and her golden hair catching the early sunlight she looked stunning.

He smiled and swept off his hat with an exaggerated bow. 'Top o' the morning to you, ma'am. The sight of you would brighten anyone's day.'

His second surprise in less than a minute hit him like a fist in the mouth. She did not answer his smile and he saw her green eyes were chill, without welcome. She held out a slim brown-paper envelope towards him.

'This is the money you've earned since coming to work here, Jim. I believe you'll find it correct.'

Sober now, he made no effort to take the envelope, eyes narrowed as he scanned her face. There was strain there, maybe some simmering anger, too.

'I'm fired?'

'Yes.'

'Because of last night?'

She dropped her gaze. 'I'll be honest with you, Jim, I . . . I'm disappointed in you. I really thought you had some kind of future with our company, but I have no use for people who solve all their problems by violence.'

'Seems there ought to be other ways,' he agreed slowly. 'But the options aren't always there, Dallas.' He nodded curtly and said, 'You should ask Lance Lattimer.'

She stiffened. 'That's a strange thing to say!'

'Russ says Lattimer's showing an interest in you, last night was his way of warning me off.' He held up a hand quickly at the look on her face. 'Ask him about it – and when Lattimer calls on you, ask him how he handles *his* problems.'

'I don't see that it's any business of yours, Jim. You'd better go now, I think.'

'Might as well. Thought Russ might've had enough guts to fire me himself, though.'

She coloured. 'Russ is young. I said I'd do it.'

'And you did.' He touched a hand to his hatbrim. 'Nice to've known you, Dallas. Guess we won't meet again.'

'Hardly likely. Good luck, Jim.'

'*Adios*.'

'Cougar Canyon? Hell, yeah, I know where it is, but no one ever uses it these days. Too dangerous.'

Will Reeder poked at the fire in the rusted grate of the old potbelly stove in the draughty old prospector's cabin. The flames threw his narrow face into relief, his eyes hard as they studied Wyatt seated opposite.

'Why the interest in Cougar Canyon?'

'Tell me what you know.'

Reeder squinted sharply, suspicious. 'Well, it's a long, narrow, winding canyon that cuts through the sierras – or used to. Mostly blocked with rubble from landslides these days, but in the old days there were so many Injun ambushes it got the name of being a hard-luck place and folk avoided it. Not even marked on survey maps any longer.'

Wyatt nodded, told Reeder what he had seen written on the pink, extra-schedule slip. 'Some instructions I didn't have time to make out but next Saturday, the eleventh, is the day something's being shipped out in secret and Cougar Canyon was mentioned. Also the name Bancroft.'

Reeder's eyebrows shot upwards. 'Was an old gold town of that name in New Mexico that folded about ten, twelve years back – or is it someone's name?'

'I believe it's the name of the agent for the Aurora bank, though the name was hand-written on a piece of card, blotting out another name underneath. . . . What's so funny?'

Reeder showed a tight, mirthless grin. 'Yeah. Arthur L. Bancroft. Must be the substitute for the local man who's been ill for a long time. Resigned and went back East to his sister just after you arrived. Knew there'd been a replacement, but didn't know it was Bancroft.'

'Something special about him?'

Reeder smiled crookedly. 'I'd say so. He's a

gambler, holding on to his job by the skin of his teeth. *And* he's the father of that young gal Lattimer set me up with in Ellis. He must've applied for the transfer. The bank wouldn't mind sending him out in the sticks away from gambling.'

'So; now we have a disused canyon, a special shipment of – something – on Saturday the eleventh, and now a banker who has reason to hate Lattimer. What's it add up to?'

'You're the one s'posed to've been doing the spying, you tell me.'

Wyatt smiled crookedly. 'Went into the repair shed the other day to see about putting a larger coach on the Madison-Ellis run because of extra passengers, and the foreman stopped me going in. They were working on a couple of coaches, replacing wheels, greasing hubs. But there was a third coach, too, one I'd never seen before. The floor was being double-planked. The carpenter was using an iron-bound chest as a saw-horse. The foreman practically kicked me out.'

He paused to roll and light two cigarettes, giving Reeder time to think about it. The older man nodded slowly. 'Strengthening the floor to bolt the chest to – but why? They don't ship gold *up* to Aurora Creek: they ship it *down* to town.'

Wyatt drew on his cigarette, nodding. 'Then there's something valuable to be shipped up to the mines.'

'Like what?'

'Gossip around the depot has it that Lattimer's working men in triple shifts at the mines. Has been for weeks. Has some big deal with a French company he wants to back him on a railroad deal, but they want to see cash up front because of his reputation for being a paper millionaire. So he has to put up his share in gold – and forfeits unless it's all paid by a certain date. But word has it the men've been working too long without a break and are about to go out on strike . . . guess they want to see some money.'

Reeder whistled, but frowned quickly. 'Yeah, well, ain't much use *paying* them when there's nothing to spend their money on up at the mines. . . .'

Wyatt grinned crookedly. 'Unless you know that there was a two-stage special run up from Madison, full of whores and gamblers, a couple of days ago. . . .'

Reeder exhaled a long, whistling breath. 'Well, I guess that'd sure keep 'em happy.' He seemed to be calculating. 'Yeah, and a payroll for fifty miners, working triple shifts for nearly a month – ought to be worth tens of thousands. . .'

Dave Denney was in a sour mood when he collected his horse from the livery and saddled up, preparing to ride out of town.

He mounted, wincing, parts of him still hurting from the beating Wyatt had given him. As he rode down Main, he looked up at the Aurora Hotel and his mouth tightened. Damn Aaron Prentiss! Got himself set up with a redheaded whore and leaves his pard to fend for himself.

Well, staying in rooms in Aurora was too blamed expensive for Denney when he didn't have any regular money coming in. He aimed to find himself a snug little spot outside of town for a spell, but it galled him some to think about Prentiss in that redhead's warm arms while he'd be tossing alone on a bed of pine needles.

'She ain't just any whore, you know,' Prentiss had told him. 'She's the one comforts the stage drivers and guards when they've got a stop-over. She hears all kindsa things, things we can use.'

Denney figured that was just Prentiss soft-soaping him. Well, let the man have his whore; *he* aimed to set himself up in one of the long abandoned prospector's shacks dotting the sierra foothills, lying empty these six or seven years past since the gold was found halfway up the mountain.

He knew of a couple of shacks still in good shape and he aimed to make himself comfortable until Prentiss was good and ready to go to work on the plan they had devised after Lattimer had kicked them out. *The son of a bitch*! Well, he was going to pay for that – and he meant *pay*!

Denney felt a little better after he'd reached the foothills. He might not be exactly built for the outdoor life – and truth was he preferred the softer, easier town life – but once, when he hadn't had so much weight on and he'd been a lot more innocent, he had spent a deal of time in the outdoors, riding line, chousing mavericks out of the brush. . . .

Then, on a few Saturday nights while hoorawing the town, that mean streak had surfaced and he had put a few men in the local infirmary, men who had rousted him out on the ranch or otherwise earned his hostility.

Then he had discovered that bending a pistol barrel over some ranny's head or kicking his ribs in could pay a lot more than forty-and-found. And for a lot less effort.

Funny, he'd worried about it for a spell, beating-up on people for money. But then he thought, what the hell? He'd beat-up on plenty of men for nothing more than the thrill of it . . . why not take a few dollars if someone wanted to pay for it? It was easy work, and he found he liked it.

Well, that was a long time ago and now it looked like he had come full-circle. That's if Prentiss's plan didn't work out, because then it would have to be back to range-riding, or find someone else who'd pay to have a man's face rearranged, or. . . .

Abruptly, he slammed the horse into the brush at the side of the trail, cursing it as it whinnied at the sudden violent yank on the reins.

There was a rider on the trail below the ridge Denney was crossing. And long habit made him hunt cover in wild country when a strange rider appeared.

The man was forking a big claybank and just the glimpse Denney had of him had set his heart racing and his right hand dropped to his gunbutt. Then he relaxed and swore softly. Hell, he was getting jumpy! Just for a moment there that ranny had looked like that Wyatt *hombre* who had. . . .

He swallowed the thought, mouth suddenly dry, as the man below started up the steeper part of the trail, lifting his face to see the way.

Denney felt his belly lurch. *By God*! *It was*

Wyatt! Well, leastways, it *looked* like Wyatt, but a cleaner, neater version than Denney remembered.

Wait a minute!

Hell, he'd actually seen this hombre around Aurora, come to think of it. Couple of days ago, just after he and Prentiss had arrived, and had been making preliminary checks for their big plan. At the stage depot – yeah! He'd seen this feller with a clipboard and papers, having some kind of argument with a redfaced *hombre* in the big doorway of the repair shed where men were working on stagecoaches.

Prentiss was talking to someone he knew who worked there while Denney was filling in time, smoking, poking about the depot in general. At the time he'd thought the man looked vaguely familiar but he hadn't been wearing a hat then and the short hair had thrown Denney off identification on the spot.

Now, with the hat on, he could see that this approaching rider bore a mighty strong resemblance to Wyatt.

No, that wasn't the name the redfaced *hombre* had used Not *Wyatt*. Denney had been close enough to catch a few words of their argument, and the foreman had growled, 'Listen, Rawlins, you're office staff and you got no right comin' in here 'less I say so. . . .'

Rawlins. That was it. Now, why would Wyatt have himself all prettied-up and be using another name – and working in one of Lattimer's stage depots after the way Lattimer had treated him and Reeder? It was meant to be a form of disguise, that was for sure – but why? What the hell was

Wyatt up to? It had to be he was planning some way of getting back at Lattimer and. . . .

He'd got that far with his thinking when he saw the second rider, downtrail, at about the same position where he had first seen the one he now thought of as 'Wyatt' – or 'Rawlins'.

Then he moaned. 'Judas priest!' he hissed half-aloud. 'I'll be damned if that ain't Reeder!' No mistake.

Well, that was all he needed to be sure the other one *was* Wyatt. The man on the claybank had stopped now, waiting for the other to catch up. Reeder was slowed down by the four spare horses he was leading.

'C'mon! We want to get these stashed in position before sundown!' Wyatt called down quietly.

Reeder said something exasperated that sounded like 'Yeah, yeah, yeah' and continued on, cussing the horses he was leading. Aloud, he said, 'I'm the one knows the way. I ought to be in the lead instead of playing at wrangler!'

'After we get the spare mounts stashed, you can lead all you want.'

'We're too damn early! There's still three days to go before the stage is due to leave!'

'You know the country, but I'll need time to get used to it, check the approaches from all directions to where we stash the broncs and also the canyon. And I aim to slip back into town and check that it's still going through, too. Could be some last-minute change of plan to foil any hold-up attempt.'

Reeder was approaching fast now on the flatter trail and didn't have to shout so much.

'Well, I guess it makes some kinda sense, but I'd be happier if we had a couple of extra men to side us. You might think you know what you're doing but I'm new to this.'

'If that canyon looks anything like the way you drew it last night, we'll manage with just the two of us. Way better if we do.'

'Sure, but we don't even know how many guards they'll be using! Christ, I must be loco listening to you. We're going into this blind.'

Wyatt threw Reeder a cold look. 'Drop out if you want – but don't expect a share. You come looking and all you'll find is lead.'

'Judas, but you're a mean bastard! Goddamn *mean*!'

'Believe it, old man, believe it!'

Crouched in amongst the bushes, one hand covering the muzzle of his mount and his sixgun in the other, Dave Denney waited until both men had ridden past and then stood there for a spell, thinking about what he'd seen and heard. He was sweating, even trembling a little.

But, by hell, who wouldn't tremble after what he had just heard? He waited a long time before leaving the brush.

10
The Deal

Russ Farren came bursting into the office where his sister was working over some papers and Dallas looked up irritably.

She frowned when she saw who it was and waited apprehensively as Russ tried to catch his breath, pointing behind him. She didn't speak but her heart was pounding as she sensed trouble.

'He's here! Well, not here. Not yet. But he's at the bank and you can bet this'll be his next stop!'

'Who're you talking about, Russ? And don't ever burst in on me like that again.'

Russ grinned, still fighting to control his breathing. 'You won't mind when you know why. . . .'

'Well? When *am* I going to know?'

The grin widened as he came forward and leaned over her desk, his voice steady and conspiratorial. 'Lance Lattimer.'

Dallas stiffened, annoyed with herself when her left hand strayed instinctively to her hair, patting it to make sure it was in place. She lowered the hand and gripped the arm of her chair.

'Lance is in town?'

'Sure is! Come in that special stage he has for travellin' around. The bald-headed gunslinger is with him, scarin'-off everyone who comes within five yards of Lance.'

By now she was standing. 'You say he's at the bank?'

Russ nodded. 'In with Bancroft. Likely makin' last-minute arrangements about the payroll. That's why I figure this'll be his next stop. I better go organize a few things, make sure the stage and strongbox are ready and so on. . . .' He paused to wink before dashing out. 'You're gonna wow him, Sis!'

Dallas tried to slow her pounding heart. Darn it, why did this always happen when Lattimer visited? She had no control over it: her face felt flushed, her belly all trembly; she could even feel a faint sheen of sweat breaking out on her body. It wasn't as if she was *really* interested in the man, not the way he was interested in her, anyway.

Russ had been pressuring her for a long time to accept Lattimer's marriage proposals but – something – always held her back. She had come close a couple of times, trying to coolly assess the benefits, but the only ones she could really see were financial and to a woman like Dallas Farren, that wasn't enough to bring to any marriage.

She didn't consider herself much of a romantic, but she felt there had to be more to a marriage than just laying out profit-and-loss accounts.

Lattimer had charm, there was no denying

that, at least when he wanted to use it. But although he accepted her refusals more or less gracefully, there had been a few bad moments when he had first realized that he wasn't going to get what he wanted, when he wanted it.

She had reared back from what she had seen in those moments, the bleak, dark flash of fury at *anyone* who dared refuse him anything.

But he had sent flowers at times, gifts of jewellery – which she had returned – on other occasions. He never wrote, except perhaps to let her know he would be coming to inspect the Aurora Creek mines and 'might' find the time to visit with her. She smiled faintly. Poor Lance! So used to having other people do everything for him that he had lost the knack of doing even the simple things.

She was still tidying her office when Lattimer arrived and she felt flustered because she hadn't quite arranged things the way she wanted. Monte held open the door, gave her one of his meaningless on-off smiles, his cold eyes scanning the office automatically, making sure everything was safe for his employer.

Lattimer was wearing an obviously new suit, no doubt tailored in New York or Paris, pearl-grey, with a diamond stickpin in the black tie, the stiff collar biting into the fleshy neck a little. He smelled of pomade and bay rum and there was a white smear of talc along part of his jawline. His teeth flashed, one front one being pure gold, said to have been fashioned from part of the first nugget he had taken from Aurora Creek. But there was a tenseness about him.

'Dallas, you look positively . . . beautiful!' he beamed.

How original, she thought behind her smile of welcome, allowing him to lift her hand and bow over it as he touched the back with his fleshy lips. Monte impassively closed the door as he stepped outside.

'We didn't expect you for another day or so, Lance.' She smiled as she spoke and withdrew her hand, clasping it in her other hand in front of her. 'You're looking . . . prosperous.'

'As usual, I hope!' He chuckled, looked around and when she gestured to the visitor's chair he sat down, both hands clasped over the top of his silver-capped cane. The silver had been worked into a wolf's head and Dallas thought this most appropriate.

She had no trouble at all comparing Lance Lattimer to a wolf. An *old* wolf, perhaps, for he was almost thirty years her senior: she could see the places where he had used dye to cover the grey streaks in his hair.

Yes, he was a handsome figure of a man, and certainly one of the country's greatest 'catches' for any woman, but. . . . There was always a 'but'. In fact, several 'buts' in her case.

'I spoke to Russ outside. He assures me everything is in readiness for the transfer of the payroll to the mine.'

'Yes, just finalizing the details, Lance.'

She spoke slowly, reassuringly enough, but she was a little puzzled by his obvious agitation which he was trying hard to hide. It wasn't like him, so she knew just how important this Cougar Canyon

Run must be: more so than she'd thought.

He smiled, spread his hands. 'I will not even ask what they are. See how readily I trust you, my dear? Perhaps you do not realize just how much trust I have put in you for this particular deal. My miners *must* have that money by Saturday night or there will be a strike. And that will cripple production which in turn will destroy my chances of pulling off this international *coup* in Paris.'

She nodded, and hoped she didn't look as impatient as she felt: she had heard all this before. 'The special stage has been prepared, Lance. I'll take you to inspect it shortly. The chest is ready with the special combination locks you had sent from Boston, and there will be six guards riding front, back and sides with a shotgun guard beside the driver. With the departure time still secret, I see no problems.'

His face momentarily hardened and then he forced a smile. 'I'm sure there won't be, my dear. Bancroft is ready to transfer to the stage whenever we wish to nominate the time. It will be best done behind the bank, he thinks. To eliminate the movement through town from the bank to this depot.'

'Yes, that will be wise, I agree.'

'Indeed. I can't stress enough just how important this run is to me, Dallas. If this international deal fails, it will be disastrous – for myself personally and for all associated with my companies.'

Dallas stiffened. 'You can't mean our stage and freightlines! You only lease them, and while we'd have trouble without those leases. . . .'

'*Every* associated company, Dallas. I have pledged much of my empire to pull this off and if I default. . . .' He forced a smile and stood. 'Well, let's look on the positive side. Come, show me the stage and the payroll chest, then perhaps we can have some lunch together. . . ?'

She could hardly refuse that invitation.

From his room in the Aurora Hotel, Aaron Prentiss watched Lance Lattimer and the girl move about the freight yard through his field-glasses. The ginger-haired whore, partly covered with the crumpled sheet, snored gently on the bed behind him.

Dave Denney watched her from his chair, his mouth slightly open, the lower lip glistening moistly. He jumped when Prentiss spoke.

'There's Lattimer. That damn mulatto dogging his tracks like a scalped monkey, too. Can see the stage and the chest bolted to the floor. Gonna be hell gettin' that free – we'll have to blow it on the spot.'

Denney snapped his head around. '*We* are? Thought you said we'd let Wyatt do it for us, let him and Reeder take all the risks.'

Prentiss was still looking through the glasses. 'Mmm. Might have to change plans some. I seen six men armin' themselves and goin' into the big shed. They have to be the guards.'

'Judas, *six*!'

Prentiss lowered the glasses slowly and turned to look at Denney. 'Don't worry about it – I got me a good idea now. We ain't gonna have to stick our necks out at all! Only thing we'll have to do is collect the loot!'

*

There were three riders blocking the trail, and they all held cocked rifles.

Wyatt and Reeder hauled rein, feeling the heat beating down from the high walls of the narrow, snake-like canyon. Wyatt tensed when he recognized Aaron Prentiss and the two men with him as the ones who had attacked him near the bank in Aurora.

Prentiss smiled, but his eyes were bleak and burning with hate. 'Mornin', gents. Fancy meetin' you here, in a canyon nobody uses no more.'

Wyatt said nothing. Reeder held his peace, too, but while he didn't know the hardcases, whose names were Skeets and Coley, he knew Prentiss and his capacity for hatred.

'Not talkin', gents?' Prentiss asked, pursed his lips and shook his head. 'No matter. Want you to listen anyways. Put simply, we're cuttin' ourselves in on the deal.'

Wyatt held the man's hostile gaze. 'What deal?'

'Aw, don't come that with me, Wyatt – or Rawlins, or whatever you want to call yourself now. Hah! That got to you, huh? Sure, Denney and me know all about you workin' for Lattimer's stageline, gettin' yourself fired for beatin'-up on Skeets and Coley here – and all 'cause you showed a mite of interest in that Farren gal.'

Wyatt was growing more and more uneasy now. At first he had figured this was Prentiss about to take his revenge for that bullet through the foot, but the man was riding down another trail, it seemed, and Wyatt didn't like where it was leading.

'Get to the point, Prentiss.'

'Or what?' Prentiss snapped, his face suddenly ugly. 'What'll you do? Stomp your foot? Cuss me out? Look around you, you damn fool! There's three cocked rifles coverin' you, each one in the hands of a man who hates your guts!'

'But you still have some use for me,' Wyatt said easily. 'You still need me for this – "deal", whatever it is.'

'Only up to a point!' Prentiss snapped. 'You agree or you die right here. See? Simple.'

'What the hell's he talking about?' Reeder asked, speaking for the first time.

Prentiss glared. 'You shut up, old man! You're in this, but I'm dealin' with that son of a bitch beside you! Now, Wyatt, I said we're cuttin' ourselves in. I can see you've gotten the lay of the land and looks to me like someone's blasted a trail through that there landslide that's blocked this canyon for months.'

Wyatt hesitated, then nodded slowly. 'It's been done fairly recently. Lattimer's men, likely. Making a clear run for the stage—' He ignored the sharp, warning look Reeder gave him. 'That's what you're talking about, isn't it, Prentiss? The mine payroll?'

'Sure it is. Denney seen and heard you two when you were bringin' in your getaway mounts. Easy to put it together, because we had the same idea. Lattimer wouldn't pay our doctor's bills and fired us. We figured to get our own back, make him pay – with interest. Just like you two.'

There was no point in denying it so Wyatt nodded. 'We're still not sure about the guards, or the time, but we figured to camp here from now until Saturday. Bound to pick up the stage then.'

Reeder was growing more and more agitated as Wyatt divulged their plans, but the drifter saw no point in doing otherwise right now. He wanted Prentiss's plans out in the open, *then* he might find some way around them.

But to make the man feel at ease, he had to seem as if he was going along with him.

'I can find out the time. But there're six guards and a shotgunner. I think he's gonna be Russ Farren, but it don't matter one way or t'other. Point is, Skeets and Coley here are gonna help you and Reeder.'

'The hell they are!' Reeder exploded. 'I wouldn't trust those two as far as I could throw a wagon into a headwind!'

Prentiss moved his cold gaze to Reeder. 'You don't have to trust 'em, old man, you just do your part and they'll do theirs.' He suddenly grinned tightly. '*Then* Davey-boy an' me, we do ours.'

Wyatt studied the man's face carefully. 'That's the part that interests me: *yours*.'

Prentiss laughed. 'Bet it does! But you gotta see you need help, Wyatt! I mean, you're goin' up agin seven armed men! In a narrow canyon where Lattimer's likely to have a dozen more men waitin' at the other end. Ah! Didn't know that, did you?'

Wyatt shook his head slowly. 'No, I didn't.'

'Why you think he chose Cougar Canyon? It's a short-cut to the mines, supposedly blocked by landslides. But he's blasted a trail through – and I've found out from a certain redhaired lady who ought to know that there's gonna be a dozen more men waitin', armed to the teeth.'

'Why doesn't he use them all the way from the Aurora depot to the mine?' asked Wyatt.

' 'Cause a dozen men and a stage in this narrow canyon wouldn't fit, that's the straight of it. They'd be strung out behind or ahead of the stage, in a thin line that could be picked-off easy. Six men – well, two can still ride abreast through that trail he's blasted and then the canyon widens some so that his extra men can either take over or join up with the original guards. Six is just right this side of the rockfall. The other dozen join up on the *other* side.'

'He should've blasted a wider trail,' Reeder put in, and Prentiss curled a lip.

'Take a good look at that slide, old man. Must've been one of his mine experts who dynamited that trail as it is. Look how them rocks're balanced. A good sneeze could set 'em a'tumblin'. They were lucky to blast what they did, you ask me.'

'All right,' Wyatt cut in impatiently. 'So the stage *must* be hit this side of the dynamited trail. To make sure we don't have trouble from Lattimer's men waiting on the other side, we can blast down the rocks and block off the trail so that we only have the six guards and the shotgunner to go up against.'

'Now you got it. I'll supply the dynamite and the right length of fuse . . . and extra sticks to blow the locks on the chest. They're combination types – din' know that, huh?'

'I guess I would've found out in time,' Wyatt

said slowly, suddenly realizing just how little he really did know.

'Well, you blow the locks and bring the payroll to a place I'll tell you about and we divvy-up.'

Wyatt smiled thinly. 'Sure we do.'

Prentiss made himself look innocent. 'Hey! We all got a part to play in this . . . equal parts, equal shares.'

Skeets, his face still showing signs of the battering he had taken at Wyatt's hands, cleared his throat. 'How you know this sonuver and the old man won't give us trouble once they got the payroll, Aaron?'

Prentiss felt every eye upon him and he smiled widely, looking directly at Wyatt.

'They won't give you no trouble. They do just like I tell 'em to – for why? Because I now have Dallas Farren stashed away with Denney . . . and they don't show, I start hangin' pieces of her all over the territory until they do – with the money. You know what I mean, Wyatt?'

He could no longer contain his laughter at the look of futile anger on Wyatt's face.

'That hit you where you live, eh, *amigo*? Yeah, this is a double-barrelled deal. Denney an' me, we not only get the money Lattimer owes us, and quite a bit more, but we get to square things with you – and you gotta stand still for it, or the gal dies. Now ain't that the *sweetest* deal?'

11
The Canyon

The trouble was there was no way to find out for sure whether Prentiss was telling the truth about Dallas.

He had told Wyatt that Denney already had the girl hidden away and was guarding her. He produced a piece of white cloth with ragged navy-blue threads along one edge. It could've been a sleeve torn from the dress Wyatt had last seen her wearing in Aurora.

'Oh, we'll look after her,' Prentiss said with a confident grin. 'But you savvy all right . . . you show up on time or parts of her are gonna start showin' up all over the sierras.'

Wyatt knew he couldn't make a move without endangering Dallas. He *had* to believe that they were holding her hostage right now and if he didn't do what Prentiss wanted the girl would suffer – even be killed. Slowly and horribly.

The fury boiled within him, but he felt totally helpless . . . for now, leastways.

One other thing he was certain of: neither he nor Reeder were going to come out of this alive, not if Prentiss had anything to do with it.

When the man rode out of the canyon, he was whistling. . . .

Skeets and Coley enjoyed lording it over Wyatt and Reeder in the camp hidden not far from the entrance to Cougar Canyon. They held all the guns and made sure Reeder and Wyatt did all the preparatory work, checking it carefully afterwards. Whenever the opportunity offered they rough-housed both men, Wyatt in particular.

Neither man had forgotten how he had beaten them up that night in Aurora. Reeder was shoved around, but not so frequently or as roughly.

They were high on the slopes above Cougar Canyon very early on the Saturday morning when they saw the dust cloud far out on the thin, overgrown winding trail.

Skeets and Coley were mighty jumpy now the time had arrived to hand back the guns to Wyatt and Reeder. They had had their fun and now weren't sure just what the men they had ill-treated were going to do. But they only talked about the dynamite they'd planted in the rock-slide and wondered if Prentiss had cut the fuse length accurately.

'He used to work in the mines,' volunteered Skeets. 'He knows explosives. . . .'

Wyatt, buckling on his sixgun, looked at the man soberly. 'You two work there, too?'

Skeets nodded. 'Yeah. We done some mine work till Russ hired us for the freight run.'

He broke off and gasped as Wyatt's sixgun suddenly appeared in his hand. Skeets fell as he jumped back, fumbling with the rifle he held.

Coley, the bigger and meaner-looking of the two, simply rolled off the boulder he had been sitting on, dropping over the far side out of sight.

Reeder was still startled by Wyatt's move and hadn't yet made up his mind what to do. But Skeets had the rifle held firmly now, brought it around, hammer cocked under his thumb, his intention clear: he was going to shoot Wyatt. And right now!

Wyatt stabbed out with the Colt, ramming the muzzle deep into the hardcase's midriff and pulled the trigger. The shot was muffled and the impact blew Skeets back against the rocks. His rifle fell and Wyatt leapt past the dying man, around the boulder where Coley had disappeared.

The hardcase had paused at the sound of the muffled gunshot and when he saw Wyatt, he dropped to one knee, firing his sixgun all in one movement. The bullet ricocheted from the rock beside Wyatt who flung himself aside, firing whilst in mid-air.

Coley staggered, grabbed his side, one leg bending awkwardly. He grimaced as blood stained his hand and then he stumbled to one side, bringing up his smoking gun. Wyatt shot him again and the man collapsed in an untidy heap, his gun sliding away amongst the rocks.

Wyatt knelt over him, cocked pistol coming down to ram under the man's ear. Coley's eyes were glazing and his mouth was slack with pain.

'Where's Prentiss stashed the girl?'

'Jesus Christ, what're you doing?' Reeder panted, running up. 'The stage'll hear all this shooting!'

Wyatt ignored him, pressing harder with his gun. 'You're gonna die, Coley, nothing's gonna change that. But I can change the *way* you die – quick and easy, or slow and mighty hellish! Your choice!'

Reeder was silent, pale, his face taut. Then his gaze went out across the plains again and saw that the payroll stage was still coming in towards the foothills. Seems they were too far out for the gunfire to have reached them, he decided. Besides which the wind was blowing towards the canyon.

Coley was gasping now, blood spilling over his lower lip. 'I dunno . . . I swear . . .' He yelled as the hot gun muzzle ground painfully into him behind his ear. 'I – Denney knows these hills. The old prospectors' shacks. They talked about one in a ravine near . . . near . . . Lavender Butte. . . .'

Wyatt glanced at Reeder and the man nodded: yes, he knew the place.

Wyatt straightened. 'Not much I can do for you, Coley. Give you a drink of water, bandage that bad one in your side, but. . . .' He shook his head. 'It's bleeding internally.'

As if to confirm it, Coley coughed and Wyatt stepped back as a pink spray erupted into the early morning.

He made Coley comfortable, but knew the man would be dead before the stage reached the canyon entrance.

Reeder watched him silently, helping where he could. The dynamite was planted, the fuse hidden, but within easy reach from where they would be waiting for the stage.

'Now we're two against seven!' Reeder said

flatly. 'The hell you want to go and kill 'em for?'

'They pushed it. I was gonna gunwhip 'em and tie 'em up.'

'That'd still've left just you and me agin all them guards!'

Wyatt nodded. 'Sure, but at least we'd know we wouldn't get a bullet in the back once we grabbed the payroll.'

'You're plumb loco if you think just you and me're gonna take that payroll now!'

Wyatt smiled thinly. 'Just watch and do like I say, but we'll have to move fast. That stage'll be here in twenty minutes.'

Reeder started to argue, but Wyatt ignored him, gave his orders crisply, said, 'Do it or ride out! I don't even need you! Just make up your mind fast.'

That shook Reeder and after some hesitation, he carried out Wyatt's instructions.

They lay in their separate places amongst the sun-cracked rocks, listening to the rumble and rattle of the iron wheels of the stage as it entered the canyon.

Wyatt moved to the dangling fuse, snapped a vesta into flame on the sandstone and applied it to the end. The smoke trail rose in a sputtering blue haze as it snaked between the rocks that hid the white thread of the fuse.

He looked up, glimpsing the two hats showing up there on the ledge: they looked real enough, like two men with rifle barrels poking through holes in the rocks, especially the way the guns angled downwards.

He picked up a cord lying beside him, tested its

tension, and glanced across to where Reeder was. He couldn't see the man but that only meant he was well hidden.

He tossed a small pebble into the rocks where he knew his father to be hiding just as the stage-coach came rumbling warily around a bend in the snaking canyon, its noise amplified by the sand-stone. Two mounted guards rode ahead, eyes alert.

He glanced at the wisp of smoke from the fuse. It was fast approaching the planted charges of dynamite, making more of a blue haze than he cared for.

Maybe the driver saw or sensed something, for he started to haul rein just as the dynamite blew with ear-cracking thunder. It hurled gouts of dirt and stones yards into the air. The explosion was followed by creaking, grinding, rumbling sounds. The entire rock-slide collapsed, blocking off the trail through the canyon, dust spewing in a thick yellow cloud. The team whinnied and reared and fought the harness. The driver stood in the seat, trying to see, coughing and hawking. The shotgun guard – Russ Farren? – tugged a 'kerchief up over the lower half of his face as the dust swirled around him.

The guards on horseback had their hands full fighting the terrified mounts.

Wyatt and Reeder waited for things to calm down a bit, the wind clearing away the dust, the horses beginning to settle now that the sound of the explosion had rolled away. Then Wyatt yanked the cord he held and the propped-up rifle up the slope beneath Skeets' hat, the brim of which was weighted down with stones, crashed and the bullet spouted dirt in front of the stage team. It set the horses to plunging again and then Reeder yanked his cord and the second rifle on the other side of the trail cracked and the bullet smashed into the coach door, splinters flying.

The bewildered guards and shotgunner and driver were all looking up towards the planted rifles when Wyatt and Reeder, faces masked with bandannas, stepped out on their high ledges, one either side of the trail.

'Drop your guns, gents! Or you'll be picked off like fish in a barrel!' Wyatt snapped.

The guards spun around and two brought up their rifles. Wyatt shot one in the shoulder and Reeder's bullet hit the other man's gun by accident or design, tearing it from his hands.

'All I got to do is give the word,' Wyatt said, jerking his head towards the smoking rifle barrels that protruded from the boulders. They looked mighty menacing to the shocked stage guards.

The rocks had stopped sliding now and as the dust cleared it was obvious the stage had nowhere to go. It was too narrow to turn around and the guards were convinced they were under four murderous guns. Slowly, they raised their hands in surrender.

The shotgun guard *was* Russ Farren and Reeder nudged his mount forward, reached up casually and snatched the 12-gauge Greener from the nervous hands. He cocked both hammers, laying his own rifle across his thighs. In moments, the guards had shucked their pistols and rifles and Wyatt tossed them far over the landslide out of sight. Next he ran off the horses and when the guards complained even under the menace of Reeder's shotgun, the older man told them if they didn't shut up they'd have to shuck their boots, too. They shut up.

The charge of dynamite Wyatt set on the lock of the paychest was excessive and destroyed much of the coach, splintering the doors and panels, but leaving the chest bolted firmly to the double-planked floor.

However, the locks were sufficiently mangled for Wyatt to kick the lid open and he stared down at the tightly-packed chamois drawstring bags. He grabbed one, surprised at its weight. Metal clinked as he shook it and the guards moved uneasily.

Then, suddenly, Russ Farren threw himself at Wyatt, grabbing for his sixgun. 'Damn you! You ain't takin' it! Lance *needs* that money and . . .'

The gun went off.

Russ had twisted it violently in Wyatt's grip and his finger had caught the trigger. Russ yelled and stumbled away, clawing at his side. Sobbing, he dropped to his knees as Wyatt threw the chamois bag aside. It struck the sharp metal corner of the chest, the thin leather ripping, glittering silver discs spilling to the ground.

But Wyatt was concerned about Russ, knelt swiftly and pried the man's blood-smeared hand away from the wound in his side. His breath hissed between his teeth when he saw that although the shirt was smouldering, the wound itself was mostly caused by the muzzle blast with only a slight gouge in the flesh where the bullet had touched.

'You'll live, Russ. It's barely broken the skin.'

He tore off his bandanna mask and handed it to the surly Farren, whose lips tightened as he glared.

'I *thought* it was you, Rawlins! Recognized your voice.'

Wyatt turned away, making sure Reeder had the others covered. 'Get the moneybags loaded on to the pack saddles. I'll fetch the mounts.' He frowned as Reeder just stared at him. 'What's wrong?'

The man pointed with the shotgun. 'We could've gotten ourselves killed – for *that*!'

Then Wyatt saw the torn chamois sack and the silver-grey discs that had spilled from the ragged slit in the leather.

Washers. Polished iron washers.

The Cougar Canyon Run was nothing more than a decoy!

Dave Denney eased back among the rocks from where he had been watching the hold-up-in-progress through a pair of battered field-glasses. He had caught the glint of silver spilling out of the chamois bag Wyatt had dropped when Russ'd tried for his gun. The sight of the flashing silver fan made his heart race and his hands trembled a little as he stowed the glasses.

Wyatt and Reeder seemed to be in control now. There was no sign of Skeets or Coley so likely Wyatt had got the jump on them – something Prentiss had predicted. Not that it mattered:

saved splitting the payroll so many times. Still, Skeets and Coley had been tough *hombres* so it would pay to remember that when the time came to take care of Wyatt and Reeder.

Wyatt came back with the getaway mounts and Denney got the field-glasses up to his eyes again. He swore softly and licked his lips when he saw three men struggling to lift the packsaddle frame across the back of the hardy little pinto pack-horse.

Wyatt ordered the guards to lie face down, hands behind their necks, fingers locked, then he and Reeder rode out of Cougar Canyon.

Now what Denney had to do was ride back to the ravine where Prentiss was holding the girl hostage and the pair of them would set up their ambush at the rendezvous where Wyatt and Reeder were supposed to deliver the payroll.

It should be easy, but Denney had a distinct uneasy feeling when he thought about the divvy-ing-up with Prentiss. He was one tough *hombre*, was Aaron Prentiss, greedy and ruthless, too. Denney wondered just how much his share would be – or even if he would get one at all.

Then it hit him out of the blue, stopped him in his tracks as he made his way back to where his mount waited patiently amongst some rocks.

Why the hell did he have to trust Prentiss at all?

Hell almighty, there was the payroll now, right in front of him.

Wyatt and Reeder rode in silence, unworried about pursuit by the guards. Sooner or later; someone would catch a couple of the stampeded mounts or the stagecoach team or the animals might well drift back to where the men were in the canyon.

Either way, they would be well out of it by then and – he hoped – trading this load of washers for the girl.

The hand-over would be the worst moment, of course, but at least they had one advantage: they already knew the washers had been substituted for the money. Still, it could be tricky, especially if Prentiss brought the girl with him as he had said he would. But there was no other way now and they had to see this chore through, whatever the conclusion.

Wyatt glanced across at Reeder. The man's face was taut and drawn, the seams in his skin filled with dust, mouth pulled down. One thing, the old man hadn't balked about rescuing the girl. He could find a hundred things to bitch about in an hour, but he hadn't griped about this.

One thing in his favour, anyway – when he thought about it, the old man hadn't been too bad at all of late, ever since he had first laid down his plans to rob Lattimer of the payroll. Hell, when he thought about it, he had been almost – mellow! Better watch it, or he'd find himself beginning to like Will Reeder.

They were riding through a draw when a rifle cracked and dust leapt from the loose upper sleeve of Wyatt's jacket.

He ducked, released his hold on the reins of the packhorse, snatched at his sixgun, at the same time jumping the claybank to one side.

Up in the rocks, Denney, flustered because of

the missed shot, only worked his rifle's lever halfway and jammed a shell in the ejector port. By the time he had cleared it, Wyatt was out of sight around an eroded wall and Reeder was riding fast for the cover of some rocks.

Denney fired at the rancher, missed the weaving figure, and half-rose for a better shot. Then Wyatt's mount skidded around the rocks behind him and Denney whipped back in panic. He brought the rifle around fast enough but missed his footing and fired too soon – and wildly. Wyatt's hurtling body smashed him down amongst the rocks and the rifle was jerked from his grip.

A sixgun muzzle was rammed into his mouth, chipping his yellowed front teeth, the blade foresight tearing painfully into the roof of his mouth. His eyes bulged in their sockets as he saw Wyatt's murderous face.

'Now, *amigo*, you want to live, you do exactly like I say!'

Aaron Prentiss swore as he lowered the long leather-and-brass telescope. He was crouched by the glassless front window of the old miner's shack, watching the entrance to the deep ravine at the foot of the giant painted rock folk hereabouts called Lavender Butte.

What in hell did Denney think he was doing? He stood, reached for the rifle where it was propped against the wall.

Reeder and Wyatt were riding into the draw, leading a laden packhorse, while Denney brought up the rear, keeping both men covered with his rifle.

This wasn't the way it was supposed to be!

The damn fool should've ridden on ahead once he was sure the others were on their way with the payroll. Mind, Prentiss had expected to see Coley and Skeets, too, but wasn't too surprised about their absence: he knew Wyatt was a hard *hombre* and it would've taken better men than Skeets and Coley to get the best of him. Ah, the hell with it, he thought now. He could kill them here as well as anywhere else. And Denney, too, while he was about it.

He glanced over his shoulder to the dim far corner of the shack where Dallas Farren was tied to a chair. Her eyes above the gag blazed at him angrily and he chuckled. She hadn't stopped trying to free herself from her bonds since the moment they had been put on after they had grabbed her from the stage depot in Aurora. She sure was a fighter. His grin widened as he stood and limped towards the door.

'Don't go 'way, sweetheart. Be back in a minute. And I'll be a mighty rich man when you next see me!'

She continued to glare as he went outside, dragging his healing, though still sore, foot. She tried harder than ever to free herself from her bonds.

Prentiss stood in front of the shack, rifle cocked and held ready for action. The riders saw him and Wyatt turned his claybank slightly towards the shack, Reeder following with the packhorse. Denney brought up the rear, holding back slightly and Prentiss frowned, feeling a slight prickle at the back of his neck.

'I dunno what the hell you're about bringin' 'em all the way back here, Davey-boy,' he called, 'but I sure like the way that old packhoss's legs are bowed under the weight of all that gold. Yessir!'

'I-I seen a chance to jump 'em early, Aaron, so I took it.' Denney cleared his throat.

Prentiss had tensed. He and Denney had been sidekicks long enough for him to tell when the man was scared – and Denney's voice was shaking like a loose shingle in a high wind. And there was something about the way he held that rifle . . . *hell*! It wasn't even cocked!

Prentiss brought up his own weapon to cover Wyatt, but the man was already spurring his mount to the side, snatching a sixgun from under the loosened flap of his saddle-bag.

Reeder hipped in his saddle, flung what looked like a chamois bag at Denney, catching him on the point of the shoulder just as he lifted his rifle to fend off the missile. He turned to ride away as the bag burst in a shower of silver and Denney lost balance and pitched out of the saddle.

That was all Prentiss saw as he fired at Reeder, being the closest, even as the man grabbed at a hidden pistol. Prentiss, unaware that he was cursing a blue streak, swung the rifle towards Wyatt and triggered.

The man slid over the claybank's back like an Indian, appearing again beneath the arched neck of the horse, Colt blazing. Prentiss ducked as splinters flew from the shack behind him. He dropped flat, levering and firing as he rolled, jacked in a fresh load as he flopped on his belly, his rifle barrel seeking a target.

By now, Wyatt's mount was past and he swung upright in the saddle again, yanked the reins and spurred towards the prone hardcase, crouching over the claybank's neck as he fired. Prentiss shot, scrambled up, stumbled with sudden pain in his injured foot, and lurched away from the shack. He crouched as he levered with the rifle butt braced against his hip, blasting two quick shots. Wyatt thundered in, Colt crashing. Reeder was firing at Prentiss, too, and the hardcase spun back as if jerked by a wire, crashing into the ground hard, rifle skidding.

Denney dived for the weapon, snatched it into a firing position by a fluke and triggered. Reeder reared up and slipped from the saddle – except his left boot jammed in the stirrup as he fell. The mount raced on, Reeder's body bouncing, as Denney reloaded and fired again. The bullet flicked dust near the horse's forefeet and then Wyatt came thundering in and Denney turned his attention to him, shooting on the run, stumbling but getting lucky.

Wyatt lurched, lost his grip on the reins and tumbled out of leather, shoulder-rolling, though the impact slammed the breath out of him. Denney worked the lever frantically, then lunged at Reeder as the mount ran past. He swung up the rifle, sighting carefully on the helpless Reeder's head, even smiling a little as he *knew* he had the man now. . . .

Wyatt rolled to his feet and, still dazed, ran at the man, jerking his left arm and yelling, causing the horse to swerve away. Denney, his face a mask of fear, spun towards the drifter and Wyatt shot him through the head even as he jumped aside from the frantic horse. It was running now for rock-studded ground between the shack and the creek. Wyatt took careful aim and shot it, the impact of the bullet from the side causing it to go down away from the semi-conscious Reeder.

Wyatt staggered to where his father lay, dirt-and-blood-smeared clothing torn, and freed the man's jammed boot from the stirrup. He finished the horse with his last bullet and, swaying, began to reload, seeing his father fighting to sit up groggily.

Reeder wiped blood from his eyes, blinked, and saw the red stain on Wyatt's side. 'You been hit,' he croaked.

'It's nothin' much.' Wyatt snapped the loading gate closed and hurried towards the shack.

Reeder, still a bit dazed, called after him, 'Wait up! I—' He paused, swallowing, trying to force out the unfamiliar words as Wyatt approached the open door of the shack. 'I guess you . . . saved my neck. I oughta. . . .' But Wyatt had entered the shack and with a feeling something like relief, Reeder said no more, fingering the bullet burn across his neck. But, *damnit*! Now he was beholden to Wyatt, and that sure didn't set easy with him!

Wyatt had the girl free in minutes. She stood warily, rubbing her slim, rope-burned wrists, hair awry, bosom heaving as she stared at him.

'Thank you, Jim. . . .'

'Name's Wyatt,' he told her. 'But you're welcome anyway.'

She was looking past him at the packhorse.

Somehow the big packsaddle had slipped and a pannier had burst. Sunlight blazed from the scattered silver and she frowned, snapped her gaze to him.

'Prentiss *told* me you were going to rob Lance's payroll in Cougar Canyon but I-I refused to believe him!'

He smiled thinly. 'We didn't rob any payroll, Dallas, all the stage was carrying was just iron washers.'

That startled her and she was silent for a time. Then her jaw tilted. 'The cargo hardly matters. If you robbed the stage, you robbed it! And that makes you an outlaw!'

Wyatt stared, said nothing. Reeder was busy mopping up his gravel scars and didn't seem much interested in anything else right then. Dallas still looked angry – and disappointed, too – opened her mouth to snap something, but, instead, said with a touch of anxiety, 'You're wounded! Here, let me look at it. . . .'

Wyatt protested; but she ignored him and insisted on doctoring the bullet burn across his ribs. 'Are you going to tell me the complete story?' she asked, as she finished tying off the improvised bandage.

Wyatt looked past her to where Reeder stood, bathing his own scrapes. 'Why don't you tell her? It's mostly your story, anyway. I just happened to be in the wrong place at the wrong time.'

'Why should I help you out?' Reeder growled irascibly, but later, when they were riding away from the ravine, he relented and told about the long years of hatred between himself and Lance

Lattimer – never once mentioning his wife, or that Wyatt was really his son.

When he had finished, Dallas looked coolly at Wyatt. 'And you – you bought into it just because you saw the opportunity to make a fast dollar?'

He smiled wryly. 'I kinda owed Lattimer something, too.'

But that didn't satisfy her. 'It's not enough, Ji— Wyatt! There has to be something here that I'm missing. I've been watching you two. There's something between you that you're both taking great pains not to divulge and I'd. . . .'

Then they saw the riders coming towards them and Reeder said bitterly, 'Now *here* comes trouble!'

Lance Lattimer and his mulatto gunslinger, Monte, reined up their mounts to a walk and approached warily. Lattimer looked grey-faced and angry, his eyes burning into Reeder and Wyatt. Monte sat his mount casually, hands resting lightly on the saddle horn, eyes alert. His gun butts, belt-buckle and conchos flashed in the sun.

Lattimer touched the brim of his hat to Dallas and then wiped his dusty, drawn face with a silk 'kerchief. 'Young Russ arrived in town with a couple of the payroll guards.' His gaze flicked to Wyatt. 'They managed to recover a few of the horses you stampeded. Russ told me what happened.'

'Yeah,' Wyatt said a little bitterly. 'We fell for your decoy.' He was surprised to see Monte grin widely, shaking his head.

'You fell all right, but weren't Mr Lat-i-mer's doin', them washers, they be the work of Mr

Bancroft, replacement manager of the-Aurora-bank.'

The man seemed mildly amused, but Lattimer curled a lip at him, raked a bleak gaze across Wyatt and Reeder, spoke to the girl. He looked like a man ready to jump off a cliff.

'Bancroft laid down the law to me when I wanted all that money moved to the mine quickly so as to head off a strike. He didn't care for the security arrangements, insisted we use the Cougar Canyon run as a decoy, while the bank – meaning *him* – would see that the real payroll was delivered on time. He personally *guaranteed* it.' Lattimer spoke the last words through his teeth, his voice beginning to quaver as some emotion made him break out into a sweat. 'I should've known better than to trust the son of a bitch! I'd had word that he'd been in gambling trouble at his last posting in Santa Fe – I thought head office must've sent him out here to get him away from temptation.'

Reeder leaned forward eagerly. 'What're you saying, Lance?'

Lattimer looked haunted now. 'After Russ told me about the decoy hold-up, I telegraphed my manager up at the mine, but. . . .' He stopped, swallowing, unable to continue.

Reeder's sudden laughter barked harshly in the sun-warm stillness. 'Bancroft never arrived!'

Lattimer's face filled with pure hatred. 'He's disappeared – with every cent of the payroll, of course!'

Reeder, still chuckling, shook his head slowly. 'Oh, Lance, you sure are in a slew of trouble! You know who Bancroft is? No, 'course you don't or you wouldn't've trusted him for a minute.'

'I never had any choice! He scrapped the arrangements I'd already made with the other manager, laid out the way *he* wanted things done and I had to go along. But, who is he. . . ?'

'Father of that young girl you set me up with in Ellis! I wrote to Bancroft and told him I believed you'd framed me and why. He never replied, but he's had plenty of time to make his own enquiries.' Reeder suddenly grinned widely. 'You're like me now, Lance, all washed up!'

'Kill him!' Lattimer screamed at Monte. 'Kill him *now*!'

'No, it's always been you and me, Lance. Let's finish it! Just the two of us. You game?' Reeder's challenge was harsh.

Lattimer spoke calmly. 'I don't soil my hands on such chores, Reeder! That's why I keep Monte.' He glanced at the mulatto, but Wyatt suddenly pushed his horse between Reeder's and Lattimer's. The fat man arched his eyebrows quizzically.

'Reeder's no gunslinger. Wouldn't be a fair shakes – I'll stand in for him.'

'I don't need you to fight my battles for me!' Reeder blazed, and Wyatt spoke coolly without taking his gaze off the mulatto.

'Yeah, you do . . . this time.'

Reeder frowned, hesitated. Then said adamantly, 'No. It's been my fight all along. You never did have to buy into it.'

'But I did – so now it's as much mine as yours.'

Their eyes locked and Lattimer snapped at the

mulatto, 'Quit wasting time! Shoot the both of them!'

The girl gasped, putting the back of her hand to her mouth, but no one seemed to notice – until Monte spoke.

'I guess not, Mr Lat-i-mer. Apart from some other things which you might not be understandin' so well, I know you just ain't got the money to pay me for this kinda chore no longer.'

'What the hell're you *doing*?' Lattimer demanded, eyes bulging with his anger. 'I tell you to do something, you blamed well *do* it, you black bastard!'

'See?' Monte looked at the others. 'Man got him a bad mouth – and what he ain't got is any honour. His dollars've bought him anything he wanted for a l-o-o-on-g time now. But no more.' He grinned. 'An' I think that be hard him to take.'

'The hell would *you* know about honour?' Lattimer demanded scathingly. 'You're only a damn swamp rat! You. . . .'

Suddenly, Monte's sixgun barrel was rammed hard against Lattimer's temple and the finely tuned hammer made a slick ratcheting sound as it cocked. Lattimer seemed to be barely breathing, his face as white as a bridal gown. Monte looked contemptuous and murderous at the same time.

'Ah! You just ain't no good to anyone. Lady, I be obliged you looks away – just for one moment, while I . . .'

'No!' gasped Dallas. 'I-I can't allow this. My God, Wyatt! Do something! He means to kill Lance!'

'I surely do, ma'am, and I'd still like you to be turnin' your head so's I can. . . .'

'*Wyatt*!'

He swivelled his eyes towards Reeder. 'I guess we can't really go along with this. . . .'

'Speak for yourself!' Reeder growled; but then he swore softly and tightened his lips. 'No. I guess not. Sorry, Monte. I'm mighty tempted and it's one answer to a hell of a lot of problems, but. . . .' He shrugged. 'Well, it *is* cold-blooded murder.'

Monte grinned, suddenly the gun disappeared. Lattimer swayed and grabbed at his saddle horn, shaking.

'Now that, Mr Lat-i-mer, that be honour. You done these here men a ba-a-a-d wrong an' I give 'em a chance to be rid of you, but they don' take it. 'Cause it ain't the honourable way, which makes you lucky, mighty lucky.'

'You – you're fired, damn you!'

'Hell, man, I quit five minutes ago. I don' work for nothin'.'

Lattimer suddenly turned to the girl. 'I-I'm sorry you had to witness this. I-I'm under a very great strain but, look, don't you worry. I've been down before. I'll come back. Just give me a couple of months and I'll have money again, and I'll see if I can get you started on another stageline and we can even talk about getting married.'

'Married?' Dallas was startled. 'Lance, I never had any notion of marrying you . . . I thought I made that perfectly clear, at least a hundred times.'

He waved a limp hand. 'That was just your negative thinking. Once I build up some real money again and you see what it can buy you, we . . . you'll cha—'

He let the words trail off as the realization came to him that he would have to bring a lot more than this kind of talk for a woman like Dallas Farren to even consider marriage to him.

'As for the stageline, Lance,' Dallas told him with an unwavering gaze, 'I saw my attorney after you mentioned that if this venture failed you would drag all associated companies down with you. There is a loophole in the lease that allows me to terminate if there is mismanagement on your part or any situation of your doing that might endanger the viability of the company. I took the precaution of availing myself of the loophole right after you left. So, the stageline will probably survive. It may be difficult for a time, but. . . .'

He merely stared, too stunned to speak. Monte touched him on the arm and the man flinched. 'Best be goin', Mr Lat-i-mer. . . .'

He shook himself, glared coldly at all of them, his wide shoulders beginning to sag despite his efforts to hold them square.

'All right!' he choked. 'To hell with the lot of you! But, be warned! You'll regret this, all of you! I'll make it back sometime and when I do I'll. . . .'

'*Go!*' Monte's gun swept up and its roar drowned the single word as a red streak leapt across Lattimer's left cheek and a dime-sized piece was clipped out of his ear, blood spraying in a brief red fan. He reeled, clapped a hand against his bloody face. Monte cocked the smoking gun again and pointed it at his other ear. Lattimer made a whining sound and spurred away, shoulders fully slumped now under the weight of defeat.

Monte grunted, unfazed by the stunned looks of the others. His dark, peculiarly lifeless eyes, sought out Wyatt. 'You be a drifter – I don' mind the company, you wanna ride along. . . .'

Wyatt hesitated, glancing first at his father, then at the girl. 'There was a time I figured I might – just might – settle down, but . . . yeah, guess I'll tag along, Monte. I have to warn you, though, I don't seem to bring much luck to folk I'm around.'

'No!' Reeder agreed flatly, tilting his jaw belligerently. Then, as Wyatt started to lift his reins, he added, with a twitch of his lips, 'But you're mighty handy to have around if your foot's jammed in a stirrup and a crazy man's trying to kill you. I speak from experience and I-I'm mighty glad you *were* around then.'

Wyatt snapped his head up, barely able to believe his ears. By God, his father was *thanking* him! Reeder met his stare squarely and, for a moment, his right hand twitched, almost as if he might lift it and proffer it towards Wyatt. But then the movement became stillborn and Wyatt nodded, his face, for a moment, seeming to soften its hardset lines. Just for an instant there, he and his father had connected on some common plane and he had actually enjoyed the feeling.

Then he turned sharply towards the mulatto. 'Whenever you're ready, Monte.'

Dallas spoke quickly as he started to turn his horse. 'Wyatt, at least let me reward you in some way for rescuing me. No? Well, why don't you think about it? And stop by the stage depot sometime and let me know what you decide? I-I'd be very interested to know.'

She flushed as she spoke, but didn't look away as he searched her face with his wintry eyes. Then he nodded, touched a hand to his hatbrim and ranged his mount alongside the patient mulatto's. Reeder hesitated, lifted a hand in a half salute as the two men started towards the blue-hazed hills.

Around the first bend, Monte said quietly, looking sidelong at Wyatt, 'I got me an idea where Bancroft might've gone with that payroll. We hurry some, we get there before he gamble it all away. Split down the middle.' He arched a scant eyebrow quizzically and Wyatt smiled slowly.

'Got nothing special to do, so why don't we check out your hunch? He might have enough left to even help-out an ailing stageline.'

White teeth flashed in Monte's face as they lifted their mounts into a gallop. 'Knew you'd know about honour, Wyatt!'

Staring at that first bend where they had disappeared, Dallas asked Reeder, 'Just who is Wyatt, Mr Reeder?'

The rancher didn't seem to hear, was gazing thoughtfully after Wyatt and Monte. Frowning, she added, 'I get the impression he's attached to you in some way.'

The words brought Reeder's head around sharply. 'Wyatt? Hell, no, he's not attached to anyone. You heard Monte – he's just a no-account drifter.'

He gazed at the dust cloud swirling around the

bend that completely hid the riders now.

Dallas was puzzled to hear the catch in his voice.

'Likely never see him again,' he added, barely audibly.

'Well, I hope *I* do!' she said. 'I surely do.'